Vaughn Christian is pissed. His alpha has sent him on a serious mission along with another shifter who keeps trying to play the mate card. Vaughn is determined to keep things strictly business between them. He's lost one mate and doesn't think he can survive losing another. But his heart and body aren't listening . . .

Finley Palmer knows Vaughn's his mate. All this cougar shifter wants is to ride off into the sunset with the man of his dreams. But Vaughn's making that almost impossible. What does he have to do to get through to the stubborn coyote shifter?

Finley is determined to fight for his love, but it won't matter if he and Vaughn don't survive this mission. At this rate, stress will either make them or break them.

On Silent Paws
Copyright © 2019 Liza Kay
ISBN: 978-1-4874-2600-2
Cover art by Latrisha Waters

Published by eXtasy Books Inc or
Devine Destinies, an imprint of eXtasy Books Inc

Look for us online at:
www.eXtasybooks.com or www.devinedestinies.com

On Silent Paws
Wildcat Hills Pride Book 6

By

Liza Kay

DEDICATION

To my readers. Thank you for your patience and encouragement!

CHAPTER ONE

"Shouldn't we talk about the elephant in the room?" Finley asked.

"The only animal I have the desire to discuss is the cougar who came into my bedroom without my invitation. *In the middle of the night.*"

Finley threw his arms up and let out a loud sigh of anguish. Talking with his mate felt like pulling teeth. Surprising Vaughn while the guy was asleep hadn't been the best idea, Finley had to admit. But he was desperate. "We're scheduled to leave on a mission in the morning." Despite Vaughn's protest, Beta Alan had put his foot down and decided Finley would accompany Vaughn to scout a secret laboratory where a crazy doctor experimented on humans. Fin wasn't sure yet if he was happy with Alan's meddling or not.

"Don't you think carrying around unresolved issues puts us both at risk?" Finley suppressed the urge to adjust himself and crossed his arms over his chest instead. Mostly because he didn't want to give Vaughn the satisfaction.

The coyote shifter already knew how he effected Finley. At the sight of a naked Vaughn sitting in his bed — the planes of his muscled body softly illuminated by the light from the lamp, a sheet pooled around his waist — Finley's cat purred in deep appreciation.

Vaughn merely raised a dark red eyebrow.

God, what Finley wouldn't give to be able to lick over the equally red morning stubble covering Vaughn's cheeks.

"Unresolved problems? Do you mean the fact you forced

your way onto *my* mission? Or the way you keep following me around, trying to be friends, although you know I'm not interested?" Vaughn grabbed his pillow and fluffed it. "Well, in my opinion the only problem is you're keeping me from getting some much-needed sleep. That, in fact, *is* dangerous because I don't think we'll get much rest during this mission."

Finley pressed his lips together and took a couple of deep breaths. Yeah, he wanted to smother his mate with his own damn pillow. And maybe punch him in the face for being deliberately obtuse. "Stop being a prick. Tell me why you're acting as though you don't know what I am to you."

"A nuisance?" Vaughn asked with a straight face.

Finley winced. Okay, that hurt. "No, my *mate*." Finley put emphasis on the last word. He took a couple of steps toward Vaughn and stopped beside the bed. "Why are you denying me? Am I so hideous?"

Vaughn laughed, but it wasn't a happy sound. A muscle in his jaw twitched. His cold gaze never left Finley's. "Don't be stupid. Just because you have a nice ass — and I admit I wouldn't mind giving it a good drilling — doesn't mean there's more between us than lust."

"So you admit to being attracted to me?" That was something, at least. Finley could build on that.

Vaughn shrugged his shoulders. He was fit for being in his early forties, but not overly bulky like Malcolm or Bailey. The light set fire to the crinkly copper-colored hair on his chest. The skin under that hair was creamy pale. "Who wouldn't be? I haven't had sex in a while, and you're constantly throwing yourself at me. I'd be dead not to get a boner around you. Is that why you're in my room? You want a cock up your ass?"

"No." Finley squinted. *Maybe.*

"You want to fuck *me*?"

Finley growled. "No." *Well . . . yes.*

"Pity. Maybe a good hard fuck would get rid of the tension

2

between us." Vaughn threw his pillow back onto the mattress. "In that case, could you please leave me alone? It's fucking two in the morning."

Scrubbing a hand through his short hair, Finley briefly closed his eyes. What he had to say wasn't easy. "Look, I think I know why you're behaving the way you do. Losing your first mate must've been horrible. I get it. But—" He interrupted himself when Vaughn snarled.

"You *get* it? You most certainly don't!" Vaughn flung back the comforter and rose, quickly closing the distance between them until their chests bumped together. Vaughn lowered his voice to a cold whisper. "You have no idea what I've been through."

A shudder surged through Finley's body. He guessed it was the combination of Vaughn's fury, the dominance in his deep voice, and the heat of Vaughn's naked chest Finley felt seeping through his shirt that caused his body to react in all kinds of interesting ways. He was turned on, for one. But another emotion, one he hadn't felt since being a soldier, pushed to the forefront. *Fear.* Finley squared his shoulders and raised his chin.

Vaughn lifted his lips at one corner, revealing longer than normal teeth. "You have no idea what losing the other half of your soul does to a shifter." A growl rumbled in his chest. What looked like pride simmered in the depths of his green eyes. "You're stronger than I thought, I'll give you that. But a good soldier knows when he's lost a battle. Whatever you've cooked up in that head of yours, if it involves you and me, you better forget it."

Finley shook his head. His mate wanted to speak in analogies? Fine. "Doesn't mean I'll lose the war as well. I won't give up on you. On *us*." Because if Vaughn didn't pull his head out of his ass, Finley had no doubt he *would* find out what losing a mate felt like, and pretty soon at that.

All emotion drained from Vaughn's face in a creepy display of absolute control. He moved closer and positioned his lips near Finley's ear. Vaughn's warm breath raised goose bumps on his skin. "You're playing with fire. You should stop before one of us gets burned." He flexed his hips, showing he wasn't as unaffected as he wanted Finley to believe.

Finley's breathing sped up. He lost the fight against his own body and lifted his hand, placing it on the center of Vaughn's chest. He felt the coyote's heart beat hard and fast, noticed the man's muscles jump under his touch. The physical pull between them was growing stronger with each passing day, though only Finley seemed inclined to admit to it.

Finley spread his fingers on Vaughn's chest — loving the feel of the scratchy hair beneath his palm — as he scrambled for words. "And if I *want* to get burned?"

Another shiver coursed through him when Vaughn ghosted his fingers over his hip. Such a light, innocent gesture, and yet it contained so much. Finley wondered how Vaughn could possibly maintain any semblance of self-control while he himself was this close to sinking to his knees and begging his mate for the slightest sign of affection.

"Then go and touch the cooktop, kitten."

This wasn't the first time Vaughn's aloofness left Finley feeling pathetic and small. He turned his head so his mouth brushed over Vaughn's stubble. His lips tingled as he sucked in a breath. He swayed slightly as Vaughn's enticing scent wrapped around him.

Vaughn pulled away a couple of inches. His gaze roamed Finley's face until he focused on Finley's mouth. Vaughn licked his lips. He slipped his thumb under the hem of Fin's shirt and circled his hip bone. Another deep sound emerged from Vaughn's chest.

Finley felt Vaughn tense even more under his hand, as though his body was preparing for an attack. Vaughn was probably strong enough to do whatever the hell he wanted to him. Finley didn't have one submissive bone in his body, was usually the one in control when it came to sex, but Vaughn's inherent dominance almost brought him to his knees.

Finley felt naughty with his still-clothed body pressed against Vaughn's nakedness. Vaughn obviously wanted to fuck him, as evidenced by the hard cock poking Finley's belly. And he felt the answering stiffness in his own pants. Finley cleared his throat. "Never been on the receiving end. Never been with a guy, either." He wondered whether he'd been clever to admit that and make himself more vulnerable in the process. But in case Vaughn grabbed him and threw him to the floor, he thought it better to warn the older man.

Unfortunately, his words broke the spell between them like a bucket of cold water. Vaughn reared back and glared. Then he grinned dangerously. "Was that an invitation? If so"—he pointed at the bed—"get on your hands and knees. I'll make it good for you."

Finley gulped. His gaze was drawn down to where Vaughn curled his hand around his bobbing prick, lazily stroking it. Finley knew if he gave in, Vaughn might never respect him. While Vaughn thought of him as a nuisance, Finley could only guess how much worse it would be once Vaughn got the one thing from Finley he seemed interested in—his ass.

Finley was too proud of a cat to humiliate himself, even for his mate. His dick and his cougar didn't agree with his train of thought, though.

"Make a decision, Palmer." Vaughn's face was as hard as ever. "I can see and smell how much you want me."

Finley shook his head. He forced himself to look away from Vaughn's big cock and crossed his arms over his chest. "Yes. But not like this. I don't know what kind of guilt trip you're on. If all you want is sex, I'll wait until you're ready to have a decent conversation with me. I'll see you in the morning." Not giving Vaughn a chance to reply, Finley pivoted and left the bedroom. Before he was able to catch his breath, he ran right into Romeo at the top of the stairs.

The ocelot shifter touched his arm and frowned. "Fin . . ." He blinked up at him with sleepy eyes. His hair was matted on one side, and his glasses sat askew on his nose.

"Don't. Please." He gently brushed Romeo's hand away.

Romeo scratched his ear. "I heard voices. What are you doing here?"

Finley hadn't told anybody that Vaughn was his mate. His friends would try to *help* him, and they'd only make things worse. As a result, his pride mates thought him a masochist and an idiot who chased after a guy who didn't like him. Truthfully, he didn't care what they thought. But he wasn't looking forward to their pitying looks once they found out his mate didn't want him. He shrugged helplessly.

Romeo nibbled his bottom lip. "You were in Vaughn's room. I usually keep my nose out of other people's business, but—"

"Then don't start. Not on my account." Finley patted Romeo's slim shoulder. "Go back to your mate. Good night." He turned and silently descended the stairs, then left the house.

The night air held a bite to it, as well as a promise of snow far earlier than usual. Walking back to his home in the center of the village, Finley zipped his leather jacket and flipped up the collar against the wind. Unlike most cat shifters, Finley loved snow and cold. Snow had the ability to cover the ugly remnants of fall under a pristine white blanket and give the world a fresh, innocent look. Finley loved to sit on his porch, either in his cougar form or snuggled in a blanket with a cup of hot cocoa—he could watch the falling snow for hours. No two snowflakes alike, just as no two people were ever alike. But each beautiful in their own way.

Finley sighed. The coming winter promised to be a hard one. No matter how determined he was to tear down Vaughn's barriers, he wasn't sure whether he'd succeed. Measuring up to a dead mate was hard enough. The thought of fighting Vaughn's inner demons filled Finley with additional dread.

CHAPTER TWO

Vaughn curled his fingers around his biceps and rocked on his heels. His fidgeting annoyed the hell out of him, and he supposed the other men in the room wondered what had crawled up his ass. He couldn't help his body's reaction to a certain kitty.

Finley's male, musky scent was driving his coyote nuts. The dumb animal scratched and whined in his head until it was next to impossible for Vaughn to follow Bailey's elaborations.

Bailey moved his index finger over a map spread on a huge table in the newly set-up conference room in Alpha Xander's house, pointing out each location of Doctor Taylor's wandering lab he remembered.

Since the good doctor had provided Richard Thoreau, the President of the North American Council, with highly trained assassins, Xander and the other leaders of the slowly forming resistance had decided to take out the man's laboratories first. Zane Taylor took advantage of desperate, terminally ill humans and offered them a cure for their diseases. However, the cure came with one whopping side effect. The treated individual, if they were lucky enough to survive, became stronger, had better eyesight, and heightened reflexes. And they regularly needed blood to survive.

Dependent on Taylor for their dietary needs, as well as bound by a contract, the assassins did President Thoreau's dirty work—namely killing everyone who dared to speak against Thoreau's plans to make himself king of the American shifters and establish bird shifters as the leading race. Bailey, who was also a doctor, had turned on his employer when he'd rediscovered his moral compass during a battle against Xander's pride.

"Right before my last mission I was stationed in a compound in the middle of Superior National Forest in Minnesota, which neighbors the Canadian border. A huge wooded area clustered with dozens of lakes." Bailey grabbed another map and placed it over the first one. "The compound consists of barracks for the assassins and the staff, as well as a topnotch, highly secured building that holds the lab."

Finley placed his hands on the table and bent over as he studied the map. "That's a trip of seventeen hours. How long are the intervals between changes of location?"

Vaughn grunted affirmatively. Seventeen hours . . . crammed into a car with tempting Finley. The guy's movement had pulled his soft, worn jeans tight around the cutest, most fuckable butt in history. *I should've gotten laid while I lived in the city. The second we're alone in the car I'll probably fuck him through the dashboard.*

"Did you listen to a thing I said?"

Vaughn looked up and knew he'd been busted. Finley's cheeks were flushed, so he'd most likely seen Vaughn drooling away. Or he was angry about being ignored. The kitty had serious attention issues.

Vaughn sighed and took a step closer. "You want us to stop in Sioux Falls. Not a good idea. I'm a wanted man since me and Romeo broke into the Council's secret prison to rescue Jules. We can take a break in Minneapolis. We'll blend in better in a bigger city." See? He was able to listen to his comrades *and* ogle a hot guy's glutes. Call him Mr. Multitasking.

Finley frowned. "Minneapolis is ten hours away."

"Five for each of us." Vaughn shrugged. "I'll take a nap while you're driving anyway, Palmer. Please don't tell me you're one of those guys who chatter non-stop during a road trip."

The only indication he'd managed to piss Finley off once again was a slight tightening of the man's lips. "Fine. We can take my car."

"Nope. We'll take my SUV. Sooner or later we'll encounter trouble. I had my car specifically converted for such occasions." He'd seen Finley's car — it didn't have bulletproof windows. Vaughn would be damned if he'd let the stubborn cougar get killed during their mission. Never again would someone die because Vaughn fucked up.

Finley sighed. "I have another car for missions. But if you insist we take yours, that's fine with me. I can be ready in half an hour."

"My stuff's in the trunk." Vaughn looked down at the map. "What kind of security will be waiting for us at the compound?"

Xander pursed his lips, then spoke up for the first time since Vaughn had joined the meeting. "Don't forget you're supposed to scope it out so we'll know what we're dealing with *before* we take the operation down." A loud crash in the corner of the room distracted Xander, and he walked over to a thick blanket spread on the floor. The alpha lowered to one knee and made cooing noises at his giggling grandkids. The triplets sat on their diaper-cushioned butts, waving their fists with happy smiles. One of the girls, whose name Vaughn couldn't remember, threw another wooden building block through the room. It crashed against the wall with more force than Vaughn had anticipated. The baby boy, Kioshi, started to cry.

A proud grin split Xander's face. "You're a strong baby alpha, aren't you?" He kissed the girl's fuzzy brown locks, then returned his concentration to Vaughn. "We need your intel so Donavan, Armand, and I can plan an attack. I'm warning you, Vaughn. Don't play hero." Picking up Kioshi, Xander stood.

"Don't cry, darling." He cradled the babe to his chest with practiced ease. Kioshi wrapped his chubby hand around Xander's index finger.

Vaughn snorted. "Yeah, yeah." He was looking forward to the attack and hoped he'd get to take an active role in it. He wouldn't do anything to jeopardize his chances.

"I mean it." Xander nodded at Finley. "Fin will keep an eye on you." He peeled a pacifier out of his pocket and offered it to Kioshi. "Here it is." Kioshi latched on and suckled wildly.

Finley groaned as though he was in pain.

Vaughn laughed. "Don't act like that's a hardship for you. You haven't been able to keep your eyes off me since I came here." He grinned when Finley flipped him off.

Bailey cleared his throat. "Guys. *Focus.* The security's tough. The compound is surrounded by an eight-foot fence. Barbed wire not included. Cameras are constantly surveilling the woods, but I'll point out some loopholes later." Bailey grabbed a pen and circled certain areas on the map. He made two big *X*s at the west and north side of the compound. "The main entrance is in the west. Don't try getting in there. That gate's huge. Just like the fence, it's live, so don't touch it unless you want to end up as a baked potato. Although the guards won't let you close enough to touch it. They're armed with machine guns. Aside from the guards at the gate, ten others patrol the fence from the inside, twenty-four seven."

"Vampires?" Vaughn asked.

Bailey shot him a peeved look. "I don't appreciate that term. I'm still human. The experiments they did fucked with my body so it doesn't produce enough new blood cells to keep me alive. Just because I have to—"

"Bailey," Xander interrupted gently. "I'm sure he didn't mean it in a derogatory way." He placed a calmer Kioshi back on the blanket.

Vaughn rolled his eyes. He didn't have time to be

considerate of Bailey's feelings. According to Bailey, the treatment also changed a person's inclination to aggression. Therefore, most assassins were powder kegs ready to go off. "Whatever. You were saying?"

Bailey growled. "The guards on patrol are shifters, though some are humans who applied for the program. Assassins are never on mere guard duty. They're called to deal with trespassers or to subdue newly turned *patients* who lose control. They're also responsible for transferring the new assassins to training facilities. Anyway, you should concentrate on the north gate. The fence is lower, and opposite the gate is a slight rise that will provide you a good view of the compound. I suggest you set up your base in that area." He marked the spot with another X.

Bailey handed Finley a folder. "Take this. It contains more info, including access codes, camera positions and intervals, as well as a map of the underground levels of the lab building. I assume the access codes have been changed since I went missing, but one never knows. Xander told me you're not supposed to enter anyway."

"Thanks." Finley glanced into the file. "I'll read it in the car."

Xander placed a hand on Finley's shoulder and pulled him closer. He moved his hand up to Finley's nape and held him. "Be careful. I don't want to lose one of my best friends and enforcers, okay?"

Finley's face relaxed into a gentle smile. The two men obviously shared a deep friendship. Vaughn couldn't shake the irrational feeling of jealousy that bubbled up inside him. He hated seeing the alpha's hand on Finley's nape. Vaughn wondered if Xander and Fin had something going before the alpha mated butterfly shifter Asa.

Not that it was any of his business. Vaughn shook himself and brushed past Finley and Xander on his way out. "I'll wait for you at the car. Thirty minutes, Palmer."

The walk back to Romeo's house was a short one. When he'd first come to the pride, he'd slept in enforcer Malcolm's guest room. However, he found listening to Malcolm and Bailey bicker constantly was immensely annoying. The two didn't live together anymore since Bailey had accidentally attacked Mal and snacked on him. Xander had relocated Bailey to Viggo and Jaxon's house. Why Bailey visited the enforcer almost daily was a mystery he wasn't interested in solving. After Vaughn had bonded with Romeo over cooking pumpkin soup for Romeo's injured mate Jules, he'd grabbed his stuff and made himself at home at Romeo's.

The ocelot and his wren mate were cuddling on the sofa, in front of a fire, when Vaughn entered the living room.

Jules grinned. "Hey!" Their legs were entwined, and their feet, clad in colorful fuzzy socks, rubbed together.

Romeo untangled himself, stood, and walked to the fireplace. "How did the meeting go?"

"Xander isn't budging on his decision to let Finley tag along." He threw himself into an overstuffed armchair. Groaning, he arched his back and pulled an embroidered pillow from behind him, then threw it on the floor with a disgusted grunt.

"He's a good choice." Romeo put another log on the fire, then returned to Jules' embrace. "Unlike Malcolm, he was in the military. And he's a much more levelheaded enforcer than our resident tiger."

Vaughn watched the flames lick over the logs. "Was he a good soldier? What branch did he belong to?"

"Army. Six years." Romeo snorted. "You don't earn a Bronze Star for nothing. I never asked how he got it, since I don't want to bring up bad memories."

Vaughn whistled. "At least I won't have to worry about the kitten doing something stupid. I just have to convince him to stop looking at me as though I'm the next best thing to cat-nip." He had to concentrate on the damn mission. People got hurt when he became distracted with emotional stuff.

"Good luck with that," Jules muttered under his breath.

"It's a crush. He'll get over it. Sooner or later." Vaughn rubbed his eyes. Maybe if he told himself that often enough, one day he'd believe it. *Shit. I don't want to have to deal with this emotional mess.* "I don't mind a romp, but that kitten is trouble." *Sexy trouble.*

Jules shot him an incredulous look. "For such a clever guy, you're pretty daft sometimes."

"What?" Romeo asked.

Jules sighed. "Nothing. Can I ask you something, Vaughn?"

"Shoot."

"Do you really not like Finley? I mean . . . at all?"

Vaughn scratched the stubble on his jaw. He'd forgotten to shave that morning. "It's not that I don't like him. It's just that his eagerness to be friends is annoying as hell." He focused on the crackling fire, having no desire to share what was going on inside of him. If Vaughn opened that particular can of worms, he'd be too distracted to concentrate on his duty to Xander. And being distracted might get him and Finley both killed. Despite the warmth in the living room, a shudder ran down Vaughn's back.

Romeo laughed. "What's wrong with having friends?"

"Nothing. But he keeps looking at me with those puppy dog eyes. He's like a teenager who has a crush on the quarter-back." Too late, Vaughn realized it hadn't been clever of him to join the couple for a chat. He always avoided talking about his private business. Well, unless he was alone with Romeo.

Jules' eyes danced with mirth. "So, give in and give him a night he'll never forget."

Vaughn smirked. "I offered to do that last night. He wasn't

interested in sex, and that makes him all the more dangerous." Truth was, he'd only propositioned Finley because he'd been sure Fin would decline and finally leave him alone if he thought fucking was all Vaughn wanted from him. Having sex with Finley Palmer was a bad idea, he just knew it. He pushed out of the armchair and stretched his hands toward the low wooden ceiling. He'd slept fitfully last night. Dreams filled with Walter had tortured him until he'd given up on sleep and cleaned his pristine weapons instead. He was desperate for that planned nap he was gonna take in the car.

Romeo scratched his head. "You two are confusing as hell. Honestly."

Jules rolled his eyes and placed his forehead in his open palm. "Men. I swear . . ."

"Look, guys, it's been nice chatting with you, but I need to leave." While Romeo was helpless at reading people due to his nerdish reclusiveness, Jules was another matter. As a former diplomat, he saw right through people's bullshit to the truth hidden underneath.

Romeo jumped up and curled his arms around Vaughn's waist in a rare display of affection. "Be careful, okay?"

Vaughn closed his arms around the kitty and held him for a moment. He liked Romeo. He really did. He couldn't fob him off with empty promises. "I'll try." Vaughn noticed Jules staring at them with wide, troubled eyes. "Come on, Romeo. I'm good at what I do. I smuggled you in and out of a Council prison."

Romeo stepped back. "We cheated death. You're my friend, and I don't have many of them, so make sure you come back."

Vaughn ruffled the short guy's hair. "I'm counting on you to keep me in the loop while I'm gone, okay?" He started when he felt Romeo's hand on his ass. "Uh . . . Ro?"

Romeo chuckled and stepped back. "Relax. I gave you a

little something to help you on your mission."

"You think fondling him will help?" Jules snapped.

"Unruffle your feathers, sweetheart." Romeo pushed his glasses up his nose. His eyes twinkled behind the thick square glasses. "I know Vaughn better than Xander does." He looked up at Vaughn. "You'll sneak deep into the lab's guts, right? And don't you dare lie to me."

Vaughn pursed his lips. "You're scary." He reached for his back pocket and retrieved a flash drive.

"Don't lose it. I worked on the thing for three nights."

Jules left the couch and walked up beside his mate. "Ohh. One of your gadgets?"

Romeo looked proud as punch. "Yup. Be a gem and find a computer wired to the lab's intranet. Insert the flash drive, and the nifty program I've written will do the rest."

Vaughn frowned. "And the rest is what exactly?"

"Break through the lab's security measures and download . . . everything." Romeo rubbed his palms. "I need more information on the compound, on the assassins they've created and trained. More insight into the inner workings of Thoreau's organization. I need . . . more." He squinted. "Get me more, Vaughn."

Vaughn blinked and took a step back. "That. Is. Scary."

"Right?" Jules sighed. "He's been acting weird for days. Please, give him what he needs. He's driving me crazy."

Vaughn ignored Romeo's indignant expression and nodded. "I'll do my best. I know enough about computers to find what you're looking for."

"Good boy," Romeo quipped. When Vaughn grabbed for him, he squealed and took off.

CHAPTER THREE

Finley dialed up the volume on the radio and shot his companion a quick look before he turned his concentration back to the road. They'd barely left pride lands before Vaughn had curled up inside his black leather jacket and fallen asleep in the passenger seat. But not before he'd informed Finley his taste in music sucked.

Finley didn't understand how anyone didn't like The Eagles. Over the past ten minutes, he'd gradually increased the volume to thoroughly enjoy the soul-stirring chords of *Hotel California*. He tapped his fingers against the steering wheel, forming the vocals with his lips without making a sound.

"Don't think I don't know what you're doing," Vaughn said in a sleepy voice.

"Shut up. This is my favorite song. You're not going out on a limb to be an entertaining companion, so at least let me enjoy my music." Finley sang the chorus aloud, dipping his head to the beat.

Vaughn raised his head to glare at him. A cute zipper print ran down the side of his face. "I hate country music."

"I don't care." Finley tightened his grip on the steering wheel. "And how come *you* make fun of my taste in music while *you* don't even know that The Eagles isn't a country band." He wanted to laugh so badly, but he knew that wouldn't win him any points with his mate. Neither would discussing the fact they were mates. Frankly, Finley didn't know how to handle the situation, and he usually wasn't one who was afraid to speak his mind.

The leather of Vaughn's jacket creaked when the man stretched his arms and yawned. "We should grab a bite to eat soon."

"You want anything special?" Finley's cougar demanded they properly care for their mate's well-being. Hell, it was tradition for cougars to hunt down game and bring it to their mate as a first gift. *I don't see that happening anytime soon.*

"Whatever comes up next. I'm not a picky eater."

"Are you kidding me?" He shot Vaughn a quick glance and saw him frown. "Romeo said you took over his kitchen."

"That's different. I don't expect others to cook as well as I do. Cooking for Romeo is pure selfishness on my part. He can't even nuke a meal in the microwave without causing havoc."

Talking about food and Vaughn's friendship with Romeo was a safe topic. Finley wanted to get to know the enigma that was his mate, so he'd use the conversation to his advantage. "I bet Romeo will miss your cooking."

Vaughn snorted. "Not as much as Jules. He has to survive Romeo's sorry attempts at creating something halfway edible."

"You seem comfortable living with them." Finley noticed a sign advertising a diner ten miles down the highway.

"Because they don't ask me personal questions." Vaughn grabbed a bottled water from the center console and twisted the cap off. "They're not stalking me, either."

Finley bit his tongue to keep from laughing. "I'm not stalking you."

"Stalking is defined as the unwanted, obsessive attention by one person toward another." Vaughn emptied half the bottle before he continued. "I'd say that pretty much sums it up."

Finley sighed. "I wouldn't have to stalk you if you weren't running from me. All I want is one decent conversation with you. But you keep snarking at me every chance you get." He shook his head. "I'm an easy-going guy, and I've been told I'm not hard to talk to. Give it a try."

Vaughn turned the bottle cap between his fingers. "We have nothing to discuss aside from our mission. I can't risk being distracted. Not while you're with me, kitten. Romeo said you were in the military?"

Although related to their assignment, that was a personal question and a chance for Finley to connect with Vaughn. "Yes. You don't have to worry about me accidentally shooting you or whatever. Unlike many others in Wildcat Hills, I wasn't expelled from my birth pride. I learned a normal job after school. I'm actually a carpenter." He smiled as he thought back on his life in Texas. "My best friend since kindergarten decided to serve our country by enlisting. I tagged along to keep her safe."

"Her?" Vaughn raised a brow. "Was she a *special* friend?"

"Nah. We were like brother and sister. So I did my stint, and then I left after six years."

Vaughn grunted. "I feel there's more to this story than what you're telling me."

Finley slowed down and took the exit ramp that led to a diner next to a gas station. He parked the car in the diner's parking area. "You're right. If you want to know more, act like a normal person and ask me." Finley opened the door and exited the car. He had to wait for close to a minute before Vaughn joined him.

The man's expression was dark as thunder. "Let's eat."

Rolling his eyes—something he saw himself doing a lot in his future—Finley followed Vaughn inside the diner. The setup was . . . weird. The dark brown tables were decorated with white-and-red-checkered placemats. A single pink flower in a tiny vase graced the center of each table. The seat cushions were pink as well.

A bear of a man stood behind the long wooden counter,

drying a glass with a dishtowel. Finley frowned when he noticed the tiny duck figurines lining the counter from one end to the other. Looking around, he saw more duck figurines on the windowsills.

At least the man behind the counter had a welcoming smile on his face that belied the sour moods of the few customers sitting in a corner booth. The five guys were decked out in leather, from their booted feet up to their thick necks. They looked out of place amid the diner's rather feminine setup.

Finley didn't mind bikers and didn't hold the same prejudice other people did about them. But the five men sized up him and Vaughn as though they were their next meal. Finley stayed by Vaughn's side as the coyote made his way over to a table by the front window.

They sat opposite each other. Vaughn placed his forearms on the table. When he lifted one hand to grab one of the laminated menus, his leather jacket left the table with a sticky sound. Vaughn grimaced, snatching the menu. "I hope their cook's better than the cleaning staff."

Finley glanced around the diner, taking in the noticeable layer of dust on the yellow lamps and the torn leather of some of the booth seats. He poked a yellow ceramic saltshaker shaped like a chick. "I wouldn't count on it. But the dude at the bar seems friendly enough." He shot the rotund man a quick glance and smiled. "Although he has an odd sense of interior design."

The man, who was probably the owner of this fine eatery, hurried over with a wide grin and a coffee pot in his hand. "Gentlemen. My name is Earl." He turned over the cups on the table and poured a black liquid that appeared to be strong enough to wake the dead. "What can I get you? It's Larry's day in the kitchen, so I wouldn't recommend the meat loaf. But so far he's never ruined any of the other dishes." He set the pot on the table, took a pad and pencil out of the pocket in his bright yellow apron, and tapped the end of his pencil against the pad.

Finley gave Earl a strained smile. When he looked at Vaughn, he noticed the coyote wasn't even trying to appear friendly. "Vaughn?"

"I'll take a water and the burger of the day with fries."

Finley thought nobody had ever made an order for lunch sound more like a threat. He smiled at Earl. "I'd like the burger as well but with salad, please. And a Coke."

Earl scribbled the order onto his pad and nodded enthusiastically. "Do you want dessert? Larry can defrost a cheesecake very quick."

"Thanks," Vaughn said in a cold voice. "That won't be necessary."

The happy grin slipped off Earl's face. "All right. This won't take long." He hurried back to the bar.

Finley shook his head. "Would it hurt you to be friendly for five minutes?"

Snorting, Vaughn leaned back and crossed his arms over his chest. "I said I'm not picky when I'm eating out, but this place . . ."

"That doesn't mean you can't be nice to Earl. What if those biker dudes in the corner are his friends and they take objection to your behavior?"

"I'm not afraid of some humans."

Finley pinched the bridge of his nose. "Neither am I, but we don't need the attention."

Vaughn squinted. "Say, how long has it been since you were last in a relationship?"

More than a little surprised by Vaughn's question, Finley arched his eyebrows. "I don't know. Four or five years, I guess. Why?" He took the cream dispenser and added a dollop to his coffee. He knew exactly how long it had been. His last girlfriend had dumped him during his final year of service.

Vaughn steered sugar into his brew. "I'm not surprised you've been single for so long."

"What?"

"Ever since we met, you've been criticizing me left and right. I can only imagine what your ex-lovers thought of that. We're not on a date. We're not even real friends, yet you constantly try to change me. Do you have any idea how annoying it is not to be accepted for the way you are?"

Finley reared back as though he'd been slapped. "I . . . I'm sorry. I wasn't aware . . ." He swallowed and lowered his gaze to his cup. Placing his elbow on the table, he rested his head in his hand, then raked his fingers through his hair. Finley groaned quietly. "You're right. But you're not making it easy for me, either. Eventually we'll have to talk about what's between us."

Earl arriving with their drinks, saving Vaughn from having to answer. Finley wanted to slap the table in frustration. "Gentlemen. Your food will be out shortly." Earl's step had a little spring when he turned and left the table.

Finley's lips twitched. What a quirky guy.

Vaughn sipped his water. "Finley . . ."

Tensing at the grave tone of Vaughn's voice, Finley met the other man's gaze. He swallowed. "Yeah?"

"I'd prefer if we avoided that particular topic until we're back in Wildcat Hills." Vaughn ran his fingers up and down the condensation-laden sides of his glass. He turned his head and looked out the window. "I can't afford the distraction. Distractions get people hurt or killed." His voice turned to steel. "Emotions . . . get people killed."

Finley had chatted with alpha mate and official pride gossip Asa, who'd reluctantly revealed Vaughn's first mate, Walter, had been the doctor at Donavan's pack. He'd died during patrol duty a year ago. Obviously, Walter's death had thrown

Vaughn into turmoil. Finley wondered if Vaughn had started to come to terms with the loss or if he dealt with it by pushing reality away.

Finley opened his mouth to answer when Earl placed their plates on the table. The burgers looked surprisingly good, not too greasy, and Finley's salad seemed fresh. "Thanks, Earl."

Vaughn grunted, staring at his plate and the huge mound of golden fries.

Earl's two chins wobbled as he nodded happily and left them alone.

Finley lifted the top bun of his burger and hummed. "Double bacon and onions. Larry might be on a warpath with meatloaf, but he makes good burgers."

"You should try it before you praise him." Vaughn popped a fry between his lips. "Fries are good."

"Are you a *glass is half-empty* guy?" Finley lifted his burger and took a big bite. The mixed flavors of beef, bacon, onions, salad, and pickles burst on his tongue. And something else. Cream cheese? What a great combination. Finley moaned happily. He hadn't realized how hungry he was.

Vaughn ate another fry, then removed the top bun and placed it to the side. He grabbed his knife and fork and started cutting his burger. "I'm a *my glass will stay empty if I don't fill it myself* guy. I haven't counted on many people in my life. Most of them let me fall."

"You're loyal to Donavan." Finley watched, fascinated, as Vaughn cut through the filling and bottom half of his burger, then stuffed a bite into his mouth.

Vaughn nodded. He shoved the bite to his cheek and talked around it. "Don's an exception. I'd give my life to protect that boy."

"Boy?" Finley snorted and stabbed at his salad. Donavan Haas wasn't tall or beefy like most alphas, but the coyote had balls of brass and led his pack with a strength that rivaled

Xander's. "What is he? Ten years younger than you?"

"Doesn't matter. I witnessed him grow up and prosper as alpha after he kicked his mother's ass. He's an outstanding man. Loyal to his pack mates to a fault. He'd never expect someone to do a task he wouldn't do himself." Pride shone in Vaughn's eyes, making Finley jealous of his mate's connection to his former alpha.

"But you're not part of his pack anymore." Finley ate a tomato slice.

"Wrong. I just don't live on pack lands. Can't stand the scenery." He hesitated, his fork lifted halfway to his mouth. "Too many bad memories." Vaughn put the morsel in his mouth and chewed slowly.

Finley nodded. "If you want to talk —"

"Don't ruin the mood, Palmer," Vaughn warned. "You've been doing so good."

His cougar purred so stupidly at the praise, Finley wanted to yank the dumb cat's tail. They ate in silence for a while, but for the first time the mood between them didn't feel tense.

Finley looked up at the sound of approaching boots, expecting Earl. One of the bikers — the biggest of them, he resembled a brick shit house — strode toward their table, a determined expression on his face. Finley cursed inwardly.

Out of the corner of his eye, Finley saw Vaughn tense, although he didn't look up from his plate and feigned ignorance.

The biker pulled out a chair and threw himself into it. Spreading his legs, he leaned back and leered at Finley. The guy looked as though he ate kittens for breakfast and gargled nails.

Finley coughed. "Can we help you?" He shot a quick look at Vaughn, but he was still immersed in dissecting the rest of his damn burger. Who ate a burger with a knife and fork anyway?

The stranger placed one beefy hand on the table and let the

other dangle between his spread legs, drawing Finley's attention to the hard bulge in his leather pants. Finley's eyes widened in shock when the man grabbed himself. What the hell?

"How much do you want for a spin with your pretty boy?" the stranger drawled.

Vaughn quirked an eyebrow.

Finley sputtered and chugged his thumb at Vaughn. "You're calling *him* a pretty boy? What are—"

"I'm not talking to you, buttercup." The biker smirked as he raked his gaze over Finley's body. "I want to know what the redhead charges for you. Let's say . . . for an hour?" He looked expectantly at Vaughn.

Finley sat in stunned silence. The guy wanted to buy *him*?

Vaughn grabbed his napkin and calmly cleaned his mouth. He turned to the asshole and said in a deadly cold voice, "Leave."

The biker didn't seem inclined to follow Vaughn's order. Finley became nervous when a muscle in the guy's cheek tensed. The stranger was human, but he was also broader than Vaughn and taller by at least an inch or so. And he had four friends watching everything from their table. Was he trying to buy Finley for himself, or for a group session? Finley shuddered in revulsion.

"I can be nice and pay for him, or I can take what I want. Your choice."

Vaughn stood in a flash, the legs of his chair scraping over the floor. "Lift your ass out of that chair and leave while you're still able to walk on your own."

The biker jumped up and closed in on Vaughn until their noses almost touched. "I have friends backing me up."

Vaughn smirked. "I only need one friend to deal with you, asshole." He dipped his head slightly.

Finley lowered his gaze and suppressed a laugh when he saw the jagged-bladed knife Vaughn held against the biker's leather-encased balls. He knew first-hand how much those knives hurt, since he'd had someone try to slice him open with one during his second year in the service.

The biker looked down as well and raised his hands. He took a couple of steps back. "Guess you're more possessive than I thought."

"You bet I am," Vaughn bit out. A low growl rumbled in his chest.

The biker's eyes narrowed, but thankfully Earl returned to the dining room. With a loud gasp, he hurried over and pulled at the biker's arm. "Ralf, what have I told you about harassing my guests? Go back to your table, or you and your guys can drink your beers elsewhere."

Ralf huffed. "Don't get your panties in a twist, brother. I was trying to secure me some tight ass."

Earl turned to them, his face deep red up to his ears. "I'm so sorry! I apologize for my brother. Your food is on the house." He fluttered his hands. "Are you sure I can't bring you dessert? Larry —"

"No, thank you." Vaughn placed his booted foot on the chair and made a show of returning the nasty-looking knife to the sheath at his calf. The move revealed the holster and handgun under his leather jacket. "I'd prefer to eat my food without some jerk offering me money for a go at my ... friend."

Earl paled. He rubbed his hand over his suddenly sweaty forehead. "Of course, sir." He pushed at Ralf and hissed, "Sit your ass back down, you moron." Ralf grunted and lumbered away.

Vaughn sat back down and, ignoring Earl, shot Finley a brief glance. "Finish your lunch. We should leave before I have to shoot someone to protect your virtue."

Earl scrambled away.

Finley shook his head. "That was ... surreal. I mean, I've

had men come onto me before, but . . ."

"You said you're a virgin."

"What?" he shouted. Finley quickly lowered his voice when he noticed the bikers in the corner shoot them nasty glances. He leaned over the table. "What the fuck? I'm not—"

"At least when it comes to sex with guys." Vaughn ate the last of his fries, balled up his napkin, and threw it on the plate. "I wouldn't advise delving into man-on-man sex with a rowdy bunch of backwater bikers, but that's up to you." He winked.

Finley's mouth dropped open before he collected himself. "I don't want to delve into anything with anyone but *you*."

Vaughn's eyes flashed with something that looked suspiciously like lust, but the man masked it quickly. He pushed up the cuff of his jacket and checked his watch. "Let's go. We have another four hours ahead of us until we reach Minneapolis."

Finley pushed his empty plate away and stood. Waving at a nervous Earl, he walked toward the door. He didn't put up a fight when Vaughn placed his hand on his shoulder and pushed him to go faster. Vaughn didn't take his hand away until they were at the passenger side of the car.

"Keys." Vaughn held out his hand and wiggled his fingers. "It's my turn to drive."

Finley handed them over and slid into the passenger seat. Once Vaughn joined him in the car, Finley turned to him. "Thank you."

"What for?" Vaughn buckled in and started the car. He shifted to first gear forcefully, pressed down on the gas, and exited the parking lot with spinning wheels and a spray of gravel.

"For protecting me." Finley turned the dial on the radio until he found a station playing rock. "Is that more to your liking?"

Vaughn snorted. "I know you could've handled him on your own. You were a soldier. And your cougar makes you stronger than the average human."

"Then why did you step in?"

"And here you go, chatting me up while I need to concentrate on the road."

Finley frowned and glanced out the windshield, taking in the empty road. "You afraid to hit and deadly wound a tumbleweed? I see no traffic."

Vaughn lifted his right hand. "Just . . . take a nap or whatever. If I'd known you'd make a big deal out of this, I'd have left you to Ralf and his buddies." His cheeks reddened.

"I don't think so." Finley smiled smugly. "Although, his nasty attitude aside, he was a big, strapping fella. Did you see what he packed in those leather pants? He was hung like a horse."

Vaughn's fingers tightened on the steering wheel and his jaw tensed. "So wham-bam you're turning from a straight poster boy to a cock-curious biker bitch?"

Finley laughed at Vaughn's disgruntled tone. "I'd rather be a cock-curious private investigator bitch."

The corner of Vaughn's mouth twitched. "Shut up and read the file Bailey gave us. This whole case is getting more confusing each day."

"Yeah." Finley snorted as he leafed through Bailey's notes. "We have a deer shifter alpha who deals with weapons, drugs, and shifters to raise money for the president. And a power-hungry, married president whose male mate is a crazy doctor with a God complex. A horde of altered human assassins are crawling all over the country taking out the president's enemies. Fucked-up shit."

CHAPTER FOUR

Vaughn parked the car and glanced around suspiciously. "Are you sure about this? This place is a dump." The neon sign glowed *m — - e-*, instead of *motel*. And the e flickered. Unless you knew this was a motel, you'd have no way of knowing from the poorly lit sign. The long, low building was painted in a dab green color that reminded Vaughn of the mushed peas Kei's kids had chugged up the one time he'd had dinner at the alpha's house.

Finley unbuckled his seatbelt. "It's a good cover. Let's get a room."

Finley's words stopped Vaughn on his way out of the car. He turned to the cougar. "*One*?"

"Don't panic." Finley growled. "I'll keep my hands to myself."

Shaking his head, Vaughn exited the car and stretched his arms over his head. When his joints popped, he groaned in satisfaction. "Fine. Did you text our location to Xander?"

"Yeah. Half an hour ago. We're golden." Finley opened the trunk, pulled out a bag, and threw it at Vaughn.

Vaughn caught it in mid-air. "I still think it's a dumb idea to give him so many updates. Doesn't he trust us?"

Finley closed the trunk and walked around the car, slinging his own bag over his shoulder. "He does. He wants to make sure we're okay."

"Checking in so often does more harm than good." Turning in a circle, Vaughn surveyed their surroundings. They'd stopped on the outskirts of Minneapolis, at a motel located in a densely wooded area. "What if your phone, or Xander's, is bugged?"

"You checked them yourself before we left the pride." Finley shook his head. "You're being paranoid."

"I'm still alive *because* I'm paranoid." Vaughn patted the front of his leather jacket, then pulled out his pack of cigarettes. It'd been too long since his last smoke. Being so close to Finley the whole day made him nervous, and he needed the nicotine to calm down.

Finley shook his head as they made their way toward the motel office. "That's a nasty, smelly habit."

Ignoring Finley, Vaughn made a production of sticking a cigarette between his lips and lighting up. The first drag made him groan. He let the smoke escape through his nose and chuckled when Finley coughed and waved his hand.

Finley pointed at a no-smoking sign on the office door. "You better let me check in. Stay out here and look suspicious while you scout the area," he said teasingly. Finley pushed through the glass door and let it bang shut behind him.

Vaughn watched Finley as he talked with the female desk clerk, admiring the man's strong back and long legs. His short brown hair was long enough to hold onto during . . .

Shaking his head, Vaughn dragged at his cigarette and turned away from the office. He leaned against the ugly green wall and crossed his ankles. Always reminding himself of Finley's obvious sensuality wouldn't help him keep his head on straight. He laughed at his own bad joke. Vaughn wondered whether Finley had ever met anyone who'd not succumbed to his charm. Something about the guy knocked insistently against Vaughn's defenses.

Although Finley was without a doubt a battle-hardened ex-soldier, he also had an innocent, youthful air to him that intrigued Vaughn. Finley was like one of those cats he shared his spirit with—a good hunter who calmly stalked his prey with patience and determination. Vaughn smiled as he blew out more smoke and flicked the butt of his cigarette away. If Vaughn weren't so screwed in the head, he'd be all over Finley like a bag of burrs.

The glass door beside Vaughn shattered, and a figure came flying through it. Finley rolled expertly to a crouch and shook glass out of his hair. "You bitch!"

Vaughn pulled his gun from its holster and ran toward the smashed door. The desk clerk came flying at him, a crazed look in her dark red eyes, her fangs gleaming in the overhead light. "Ah fuck." He'd never heard Bailey mention female vamps. He knew from Xander that the assassins were damn strong and hard to defeat for a full-grown alpha. The best way to end them was to put a bullet through their head. Before Vaughn had time to raise his gun, she barreled into him and knocked him to the ground.

"Fucking blood-sucking bitch!" Vaughn cocked his arm and punched her in the face.

She merely snarled and ringed her hands around his neck.

Vaughn pressed the pistol against her belly, intending to blow a hole through her intestines, when Finley appeared behind her and gripped her in a headlock. He pulled the woman off Vaughn and grappled with her, but it was obvious the vamp was an even match for the shifter. She shrieked and snapped her sharp teeth at Finley's neck.

From his vantage point on the ground, Vaughn tried to get a shot at her. Unfortunately, she was trying to snack on Finley, who managed to keep her away from his jugular with some difficulty.

Eventually Finley drew his knife. He sliced through the air in an arc and caught the woman's chest. The blade ripped through her skintight garments. Although blood splattered over Finley's clothes and face, the injury didn't seem to slow the vamp down.

She delivered a round-house kick with her heeled foot and kicked the knife out of Finley's hand. She snickered and curled her taloned fingers into claws. "Kitty, kitty . . ." When Finley inched toward Vaughn's sprawling body, she snapped her gaze back and forth between them.

"Shit," Vaughn hissed. He fired as she turned from Finley to attack him instead. His shot hit her in the shoulder. Although she stumbled for a second, she descended on him like a Fury.

Vaughn threw the gun toward Finley, then brought his arms up to defend himself against her sharp nails and fangs. "Get off me, you crazy-ass bloodsucker!" Ignoring his command, she straddled him. At the sound of a cocking gun, Vaughn froze and lifted his gaze.

Finley held Vaughn's gun in one hand, supporting it with the other. He panted for breath. "Release him."

She laughed and nudged Vaughn in the chest with something hard. When he turned his head, he saw it was another gun. And she had it pointed directly at his heart. Not even a shifter could survive such a wound. Vaughn swallowed. Sweat broke out on his forehead. "Finley." When nothing happened, Vaughn glanced toward the man.

Finley's hands were shaking. He was pale as a sheet, and his eyes . . . he looked as though he was somewhere else. This was the worst moment ever for a panic attack, or a flashback, or whatever else Finley might be going through.

"Palmer, dammit! *Shoot* her!"

The witch cackled. "He can't. The kitty's afraid." Her eyes gleamed with triumph. Vaughn used her distraction to reach for the knife strapped to his leg. She lifted the gun from Vaughn's chest and pointed it at Finley.

"No!" Vaughn shouted for Finley to shoot, but it was too late. The discharge of the bitch's gun nearly rendered him deaf. Vaughn watched in shock as the bullet slammed into

Finley's chest and flung him backward. Finley dropped to the ground like a stone.

Vaughn tightened his grip on the knife and plunged it through the woman's neck.

Her eyes widened. The gun slipped from between her fingers and clattered against the gravel. She lifted her hands to her neck. A gargling sound left her throat. Blood gushed from the wound and seeped between her fingers.

When Vaughn pushed her off him, she slumped to the ground. She wouldn't be getting up again. Scrambling to his hands and knees, Vaughn crawled over to Finley. The man's eyes were closed. "Fin! You stupid fucking asshole." When he reached him, he ran his hands over Finley's chest, searching for the wound. "Please, don't do that to me. Don't you dare die on my watch!"

Finley groaned. His lids fluttered open. "Fuuuuck. I'd forgotten how much this shit hurts."

"What?" Vaughn was going out of his mind with panic. He found the zipper of Finley's jacket and yanked it open. He blinked when he saw the torn shirt where the bullet had hit Finley's chest right over his heart. He found no blood. Cursing, he pushed up Finley's shirt and found a protective vest underneath. "You . . . when . . ."

Finley touched the back of his own head and winced. "Before I climbed in your car this morning. I'm not dumb."

"Fuck!" Vaughn punched Finley's left shoulder. He sobbed. "I thought . . ."

Finley let out a pained groan. "Whoa. Watch it. I'm not dead, but being shot hurts like a bitch even with the vest."

"You deserve it. I thought you were dead! Shot in the chest . . ." Vaughn pushed off the ground and ran his hands through his hair. "Why the fuck did you hesitate? You should've pulled the trigger. Instead you put us both in danger."

Finley rolled to his side and sat up, pressing a hand against his chest. He grimaced. "I couldn't do it."

"Why? She'd have torn out your jugular without regret and worn it as a necklace for shits and giggles." Vaughn threw his arms into the air and stalked over to the dead assassin. Kneeling beside her, he searched her body and piled everything he found beside her. They might need the weapons later.

"I don't want to talk about it." Finley scraped himself off the ground and limped toward him.

"You *have* to. Whatever it is, this issue makes you a risk in battle." Vaughn checked the vamp's gun and put the safety on. "I need to know I can count on you to keep yourself and me safe. Mostly yourself. I can't concentrate when I'm worrying about you." When he looked up, he found Finley glaring at him.

"So *I* have to lay my cards on the table but *you* can stay silent?" He turned and walked toward the trashed office. "I'll see what happened to the real clerk. I wonder how she found us in the middle of nowhere."

Vaughn shook his head. When he was done relieving the woman of her arms, he grabbed her by the wrists and dragged her dead body between the trees. Roughly twenty feet behind the tree line, the ground sloped into a ravine. Vaughn gave the body a kick and watched as she rolled down into the ravine. As he came out of the woods, Finley hurried down the stairs from the office, holding both their bags. His face was a mask of stone.

"The clerk's dead. She tore out his throat and snacked on him. That place doesn't have any cameras. We should leave." Finley threw the bags onto the backseat of the car and slid into the passenger seat.

Vaughn joined him in the car and winced when the blood on his clothes left smudges over his baby. He'd had to invest in an expensive interior cleaning after Jules' rescue a couple of months ago. He sped off. "Where to? We're a mess."

Finley wriggled around and shrugged out of his jacket. "I know a place in Minneapolis." His shirt was, save for the hole in it, mostly intact. He pulled it over his head and rubbed the fabric over his bloody face. Dog tags dangled around his neck and stuck to his sweaty chest. "They won't ask questions."

"Why?" Vaughn grabbed the water bottle from the center console and tossed it onto Finley's lap.

"Because with the right cash they don't look too closely. I stayed there before." Finley poured some water onto the shirt and cleaned his face. His fingers shook. "You can park in the underground garage and wait for me while I secure a room."

Vaughn snorted. "Yeah. Because the last time I let you loose to get us a room we didn't nearly die."

"You'll never let that go, huh?" Finley grinned. Still, his falsely upbeat mood didn't conceal the pallor of his face.

"The memory is still kinda fresh." Vaughn gripped the steering wheel tighter. He couldn't believe the dumb kitten had risked his life over a vampire assassin bitch. Finley was a soldier. He'd probably killed before, both in the military and as an enforcer for Xander. He was so unlike Walter. Fin was supposed to play it safe.

Vaughn tried to chase the thought away, but once in his head, the memory wouldn't leave him. Walter hadn't been trained for battle. As a doctor, he'd despised fighting and bloodshed in general, even in the rare cases when it had been necessary to defend the pack. Walter had never concealed his dislike of Vaughn's part-time status as a pack fighter.

Walter, the pacifist, had died by a poacher's bullet. Vaughn had thought Finley capable of defending himself because he was battle-trained. Tonight, he'd almost lost him. *Like I lost Walter. It's the same all over again, and here I am trying to convince myself I don't care about the kitten. Shit.*

Finley cleared his throat. "At the next intersection turn

right and drive into Minneapolis." The sharp sound of Velcro releasing sounded in the car when Finley loosened his bullet proof vest and threw it onto the backseat. "You're awfully quiet. Look, I'm sorry. I . . ."

"If you tell me yours, I'll tell you mine." Vaughn winced, but he didn't take the spontaneous words back. If he wanted to protect Finley, he had to unveil the man's inner demons. However, he knew he had to give a little to get something from Finley. He shot the man a quick glance and found Finley staring at him with wide eyes.

"Are you sure?" Fin rummaged in the bag between his feet and retrieved a tank top that he yanked over his head.

No. Growling, Vaughn returned his focus on the road. "Yeah."

Finley was quiet for so long Vaughn didn't expect him to answer. Then, in a quiet, detached voice, he said, "I killed a woman."

Vaughn had expected something along those lines. "I'm listening." He shot Fin a quick look and saw him clutch his tags.

"My six years were up. I actually considered re-enlisting, since my girlfriend back home had left me for someone else, someone who wasn't gone all the time. Nothing to come back home to. I was in Afghanistan." Finley emptied the water bottle.

"What happened?"

Finley brought his foot up against the dashboard and placed his elbow on his knee. "We were patrolling a market. Everything was calm. We hadn't gotten any hints from our local allies that something might go down." He laughed suddenly, but it wasn't a happy sound. "All hell broke loose. Men with machine guns stormed the market, firing into the crowd. They weren't interested in us, but some of my comrades went down in the first couple of minutes." Finley raised a hand to his mouth and rubbed over his lips. "Of course we fought back. A bomb went off, and I was disoriented. My ears were ringing, and I . . . it was pure chaos."

Vaughn slowed the car and pulled over, parking on the side of the road. Without looking at Finley, he held out his hand palm up and waited.

Finley grabbed his hand like a lifeline and squeezed tight with his cold-as-ice fingers. He linked their fingers and tugged their joined hands in his lap. He was shaking, and the scent of nervous sweat perfumed the air. "I saw a group of women. They were arguing in the middle of the chaos and destruction. I ran over to them. My intent was to guide them somewhere safe . . . protect them." He took a deep, shuddering breath. "When I came closer, I saw one of them had a bomb strapped to her waist. She was holding the other women at gunpoint so they wouldn't run away. I stopped and shouted at her to drop the weapon." Finley rubbed at his eyes.

Vaughn slid closer and placed his second hand on Finley's. "You don't have to go on if it's too much," he whispered.

Finley shook his head rapidly. "You're right. You deserve the truth. She . . . she turned and grinned at me. Just grinned. It was the expression in her eyes, the crazy gleam. I knew she'd . . ." He swallowed, his Adam's apple bobbing. "I shot her before she had the chance to blow us to hell. Later I found out the belt held enough explosives to cremate everyone in the whole marketplace."

"Romeo . . ." Vaughn cleared his throat. "He said you got a Bronze Star."

Finley nodded, looking down at their linked hands. "I kept fighting after I shot her. Killed most of the other attackers and dragged my comrades who couldn't walk anymore to safety. I hadn't been wounded during the fight, and my shifter genes helped me carry them. They thought I deserved a reward."

"Well, you did!" Vaughn cupped Finley's cheek and forced

him to meet his gaze. "You deserved it. You saved many lives that day."

Finley blinked rapidly. "Two of my team died. My best friend Sheila was one of them. When I found her . . . her death pulled the rug out from under my feet. I'd never killed a woman in battle before, and I lost my best friend the same day. I came home a broken man and I left the service because my whole reason for enlisting had been to protect Sheila." Finley shook his head. "I'm sorry for fucking up earlier. I can't promise it won't happen again."

"Don't fret. Now that I know, I'll deal with whatever woman comes at us." Vaughn freed one of his hands and brushed it through the sweaty hair at Finley's temple.

Finley looked at him. His expression was haunted, pained, showing a loss he hadn't yet dealt with. Vaughn knew what that looked like, because he saw the same expression in the mirror every morning. He felt closer to Finley than he'd ever felt to another person before. It was a dangerous feeling, a flutter in his chest, as though his heart was skipping a beat, not to mention the tingly feeling in his hand where Finley held it.

Finley cleared his throat and broke the connection. He freed his hand and opened the car door. "Do we have more water in the trunk?"

"Yeah." Disappointment slammed into Vaughn like a fist to his gut. He wasn't sure what he'd hoped would happen, but he'd expected something. "Grab one for me as well, please." Closing his eyes, Vaughn leaned back against the headrest and cursed quietly. Finley had opened himself. Now it'd be his turn.

Finley returned and slammed the door. He handed Vaughn one bottle, then opened the other and gulped down half of it He brushed the back of his hand over his mouth. "You don't have to tell me right away."

"What?"

Finley shrugged. His wide shoulders were perfectly highlighted by the clingy tank top that snuggled against his sleekly muscled, smooth chest. "I've been waiting for you to talk with me for days. But I don't want you to feel pressured, or feel you owe me anything. I want you to tell me when you're ready. When it's *your* decision, not when it's part of some deal."

There was that fluttery feeling again. This time it spread from his chest down to his belly. Maybe Larry's burger hadn't been so good after all. That had to be it. The food.

"Well, this is posh." Vaughn studied himself in the mirrors lining the walls of the elevator and found he looked like death warmed over. Maybe worse. His clothes were torn and dirty. His unruly red corkscrew curls were a disaster. The blood on his face didn't help, either. He brushed a hand through his hair, noticing the silver strands at his temples that seemed to multiply every day. Maybe he should return to a buzz cut.

Finley leaned casually against the wall. He'd covered his tank top with a sweater from his bag. "I booked us a room with two beds. Do you want to shower first while I order room service?"

"Yes, please. The bitch's blood smells rank, like a dead racoon."

"I forgot to ask. Did you find anything on her aside from weapons?"

Vaughn patted the pocket of his jacket. "Cell phone. I'll connect it to my laptop and see what I can find. Romeo and Jules supplied me with a handy program." Romeo was one of the best hackers Vaughn had ever known. The elevator dinged softly, and the doors slid open with a whisper-soft sound. Their steps on the thick gold and blue carpet were also whisper-soft as they left the elevator and padded toward their room. Vaughn took in the pictures that hung on the walls. "How much did one night cost you?"

"Two-fifty. You're not a cheap date, that's for sure."

Vaughn snorted. "Would it make you feel better if I paid for dinner?"

"I don't know." Finley stopped in front of a door and held the card against the scanner. Their gazes met. "Did you plan to cause another scene so you get the food comped?" He winked and pushed the door open.

"*You* caused the scene, *pretty boy*." Vaughn passed him and stalked straight to the bed closest to the door. His choice obviously didn't slip Finley's attention, because he made a disgruntled noise.

"What are you hungry for?"

Vaughn tensed and stopped in the midst of unzipping his bag. His body responded to the probably unintentional innuendo in the most annoying way. "Pick something." He unzipped his bag forcefully, grabbed a change of clothes, and vanished inside the bathroom without looking at Finley.

The damn bathroom was marble and gold. It reminded him of his bathroom back home. His pack home, not the shabby apartment in Sioux Falls. Vaughn yanked his shirt over his head, balled it up, and stuffed it into the trash. The pants might be salvageable, so he folded them to bag later. He dropped his boxers and entered the shower then turned the water to hot.

A moan escaped him when the hard splash hit his back. Vaughn placed his underarms against the wall and rested his forehead on them. He shuffled around until the water hit his tense neck muscles. Opening his eyes, he saw his traitorous prick bobbing between his legs. "Forget it, buddy."

He hadn't had sex since Walter. Hell, he'd never in his life had sex with anyone but his late mate. He'd been so young and naïve when they met. What he wouldn't give for five more minutes with the old guy. Not to have sex, but to clear the air. To say goodbye properly. To be forgiven. Vaughn glanced at the closed bathroom door.

"I killed my first mate. Why does fate think I deserve a second one?" Vaughn shook his head and pressed the soap dispenser attached to the wall. He worked up a lather and quickly washed the grime of the day away. Pink water gurgled down the drain, thanks to the earlier blood spray. After he'd washed his hair and body twice, Vaughn cut off the water and stepped out onto the plush bathmat. He snatched a heated towel from the rack and fixed it around his hips.

Finley knocked at the door. "Vaughn? Do you have a first-aid kit in your bag?"

"Sure." Cold gripped his heart. "What do you need?" He yanked the door open. Finley stood there, shirtless, his boxer briefs embellished with cats and milk bowls. *Shit and damnation.* "Where are you hurt?"

"I might need some stitches." Finley pointed at his arm.

Vaughn was too distracted by the purple bruise on Finley's pectoral where the bullet had hit him. And the scars. Three long slashes—claw marks—marred the smooth, tanned skin of his chest. A healed bullet wound scarred his shoulder. Blinking rapidly, Vaughn pushed past the man and hurried to his bag. "Sit your ass down."

Finley chuckled and plopped onto the edge of the bed. "I know. I'd have more scars if it wasn't for my shifting abilities. I caught a bullet to the shoulder during the service."

"You never take off your tags, huh?"

"They're part of my life. They help me remember my path as much as my scars do. The claw marks, those'll vanish with time. I had a disagreement with Bailey a couple of months ago."

"What?" Vaughn snatched the first aid kit from his bag and knelt in front of Finley. "He *hurt* you? I'll fucking kill him when we get home," he muttered under his breath. "Show me your arm." He knee-walked between Fin's spread legs, trying to ignore his manly scent and the warmth of his thighs — and the ridiculously cute boxers.

Fin stretched his arm and smiled. "Bailey was protecting Malcolm, weird as it sounds. They're both huge. It was the craziest shit. Happened right after Bailey wrestled Malcolm to the ground and snacked on his jugular."

Frowning, Vaughn inspected the cut on Finley's underarm. That was too deep for butterfly bandages. "You're right. You need stitches. Let me numb the area."

"Don't. I can't afford a muddled brain," Finley said quietly. "I wonder . . . if Bailey and Mal are mates."

Mates. Why does every conversation come back to that one topic? Ignoring the twinge in his gut, Vaughn iced Finley's wound and waited. "I don't know them well enough to take a guess. They sure as hell bicker like an old married couple, but I have trouble imagining them as an item."

"Crazier pairings have happened." Finley's gaze met his. "I respect your wish to skirt that subject. I'm sorry. Stitch me up so I can take a shower too. I reek."

Vaughn snorted. "I had no idea female vampires existed. I wonder if Bailey heard of them. But . . ." He carefully threaded the needle. "We shouldn't contact anyone after the ambush at the motel. If our cells aren't bugged, we have a mole in the pride. In the inner circle no less, because I can't imagine Xander discussing our whereabouts with anyone."

Finley cursed quietly. "Shit. Maybe Raine?"

Raine was a harpy shifter who'd worked as a spy on behalf of French Council President Armand Dubois. Armand was an old acquaintance and ex-lover of Jules. The President claimed he wanted to end Thoreau's reign of terror as much as Xander. They considered him an ally. "I don't like Raine. He's got an attitude, and he was responsible for Jules being captured and tortured. But he left the pride today and accompanied

Armand to Donavan's. How do you feel about Armand?"

"Not sure." Finley shook his head.

"He's a president. What if he's in cahoots with Thoreau and he's taking advantage of his friendship with Jules to undermine us?" Vaughn started to stitch up Finley's wound.

Finley pursed his lips. "Let's withhold our position from now on. We had enough surprises today."

CHAPTER FIVE

Finley awoke to a dark hotel room. Thanks to being a cat shifter, his night vision was excellent, but lying on his side facing the wall didn't help. Something must've disturbed his sleep. Ever since his time in the human military, he'd been a light sleeper.

Then he heard it. Heavy breathing. Rustling sheets. A sigh. Finley wondered what Vaughn was doing. Maybe he was having a bad dream? Just when Finley considered getting up and waking Vaughn, the sound of sheets rustling over skin reached his ears. Two feet touched the carpet, indicating Vaughn was awake and on the move.

Before Finley had the chance to turn and ask what was going on, his blanket was lifted and a naked body snuggled up behind him.

Gasping, Finley flipped over. "What the—" The next second, Vaughn's lips met his in a sloppy, wet kiss. Vaughn tasted like pasta sauce and the cigarette he'd smoked before bed. Although Fin thought it a nasty habit, he ignored the bitterness and returned the kiss. Who knew when the next chance would present itself? He opened his lips in a blatant invitation.

Vaughn burrowed his fingers in Finley's hair and held on tight while he slid his tongue into Finley's mouth.

Fin groaned. He didn't know what was going on, but he didn't have it in him to care. Finley was tired of Vaughn pushing him away, of waiting for the smallest sign Vaughn felt the pull between them. His cougar was damn tactile and needed the closeness, so Fin planned to enjoy the kiss as long as it lasted.

Vaughn's hairy body was hard and firm against his. Although it was a new sensation for Finley, who was used to the soft curves of women, he relished it. Fin closed his eyes when Vaughn pushed him onto his back and rolled on top of him. He wanted to open his legs for Vaughn to fall between them, but instead Vaughn straddled him. Fin opened his eyes at the unexpected sensation of Vaughn's naked butt and balls against his belly.

Fin broke the kiss, panting for breath. "Babe?" He grabbed Vaughn's biceps and squeezed them. "What's going on?"

Vaughn's green eyes swam with moisture.

The sight broke Fin's heart.

"Bad dream. I thought the bitch had killed you." Vaughn's voice broke on the last word, and he lowered his head and hid his face against Finley's neck. His hold on Finley's hair tightened. "Without the vest, she would've taken you from me. You can't . . . I need . . . Not again. I can't go through this again."

"What do you need?" Fin slung his arms around his mate's broad back and rubbed his sweat-slick skin. Vaughn's breath against his neck sent a shiver through his body and blood pooled in his groin.

"I need to feel you're alive." Vaughn licked Fin's jawline, then sucked hard on his neck. "I need you to promise you'll be more careful, my stalker. I thought . . . if I kept my distance . . . I could keep you safe."

Fin tipped his head back to allow Vaughn more access, still caressing his back and sides. The man's muscles felt divine under his fingers. "Shh. I'm here." How was he expected to hold a conversation, soothe Vaughn's fears, while the man drove him crazy with teasing nips to his neck?

"Not good enough," Vaughn whispered. He untangled

one hand from Finley's hair and pushed it between their bodies. When his knuckles brushed against Finley's cock, Fin gasped and arched his back.

"We can't—" Fin was silenced with an eager kiss.

"Shut up." Vaughn wrapped his hand around Fin's cock and stroked up and down at an admittedly awkward angle. "We both need this."

Despite the weird situation, feeling his mate's hand on his shaft still felt good, so it wasn't long before Fin was hard as a rock. He pushed through Vaughn's tight grip, sucking and nibbling on his mate's lip. "Fuck." Fin hadn't been touched by anyone in months. With the pride in upheaval, he hadn't had time to go to a bar and find a hook-up. And the fact it was Vaughn pleasing him had him dangerously close to the edge in an embarrassingly short time.

"Do you want to?" Vaughn sat up. He placed one large hand in the middle of Fin's chest and held Fin's cock with the other one. When Vaughn pressed the crown of Fin's cock against his hole, Fin's eyes snapped wide.

"No, wait!" Fin placed his hands on Vaughn's hips and hissed. "You're slick. How—"

"Played with myself while you were asleep until I couldn't think of anything but touching you. I need it bad, Palmer. Don't have the patience to prep a virgin, so you'll have to do me." Vaughn's face showed a mix of emotions. Determination. Vulnerability. Fear.

Although Fin related to all of those, he didn't think sex was the solution to any of their problems. But when Vaughn slid down his dick, his protest died on his lips. He wasn't a stranger to sex, but he'd never had anal sex with any of his female lovers. Vaughn's ass was incredibly tight and hot around his shaft. When he was as deep as possible, Fin took a shuddering breath. "Holy shit." Fin mewled—fucking mewled like a kitten—trying to rein in the orgasm threatening to overwhelm him. *God, please don't let me embarrass myself.* "You're perfect. I've never . . ." He swallowed. Fin slid his hands up and down Vaughn's sides, admiring the play of tight muscles under pale skin. He raked his fingers through the red pelt on Vaughn's chest.

"Never?" Vaughn's voice had dropped an octave to a deep and throaty rumble, a promise of naughty pleasure. He sat still, probably adjusting to the penetration, but followed the scars on Fin's chest with his fingertips. He briefly brushed his fingers over Fin's dog tags.

"Never felt so connected to anyone." Fin didn't care if that statement made him weak in his mate's eyes. Vaughn had to live with the truth. He reached up and wrapped one hand around Vaughn's nape. He pulled Vaughn down and into a gentle kiss.

Vaughn's lashes fluttered. A soft sigh escaped his lips. "Incredible." Wonder shone in Vaughn's eyes. He rocked his hips, slowly at first but gaining speed as they became more comfortable with each other.

"Like this, baby?" Fin planted his feet on the bed and pushed up with his hips.

"Yes. I need to feel you. All of you. Show me you're really here with me."

Fin cupped Vaughn's face and never broke his mate's gaze. Vaughn was absolutely beautiful. A strong, red-headed warrior with the chiseled body of a god, he was showing a level of vulnerability Fin hadn't thought possible. For the first time, Fin glimpsed a sign of the gentle, bruised soul behind Vaughn's brash, standoffish exterior.

"I've got you." Fin repeatedly brushed his fingers through Vaughn's unruly curls.

Vaughn gasped. "Damn, Palmer. Should've known you'd turn this into more than . . ." He writhed against Fin with fluid, forceful motions, like a dancer caught in a choreography of pleasure. He raked his nails down the middle of Fin's chest, his face twisted in pleasure.

Fin snarled. "More than a fuck?" His balls tightened at the sting of pain. He caught Vaughn's lips in a hard kiss that was teeth and tongues. He tasted copper but was too far gone to worry about it.

"Yes. Harder." Vaughn's canines were longer than normal. Blood smudged his lips.

Fin grunted when Vaughn bounced up and down with a painful intensity. When Fin snapped his hips to meet Vaughn's ass, he must've hit the right angle, because Vaughn let out a deep, long groan Fin was sure echoed through the whole hotel. "That your spot?" He memorized the angle and flexed his hips repeatedly.

"Close!" Vaughn focused on Finley and didn't break the gaze. Wonder shone in Vaughn's green eyes when his body stiffened and warmth hit Finley's chest. Vaughn's low, drawn-out moan sounded soul-deep, as though it was the result of months of suppressed pain and sorrow.

Through it all, Finley held his mate to his chest. The tightness of Vaughn's channel, the spicy scent of sweat and spunk, as well as the shudders that ran through Vaughn's strong body, turned his cougar into a contented, purring ball of happiness, although he hadn't found his own release.

When Finley felt something wet on his neck, he cupped Vaughn's face and lifted it. "Baby?"

A tear ran down Vaughn's face. "I'm so sorry."

Concerned, Fin purred, hoping to soothe his mate's nerves. "Shh." He kissed Vaughn's cheeks, lips, and eyes, nuzzled and patted him.

"Sorry." Vaughn sagged against his chest as racking sobs shook his whole body.

Finley held the back of Vaughn's head and pressed his face against the crook of his neck. "You're safe. I'm safe. Nobody can hurt us."

"*I* did." Vaughn sniffled. "I *do*. Hurt you. And you can't promise that. Fuck, I didn't mean to break down."

Finley fought against his own tears at the pain and fear in Vaughn's voice. "Look . . . I've never considered myself a great catch. I don't own much aside from my house and a couple hundred dollars in the bank. I . . . I've never been in love. But I can promise you one thing. Allow me to hold you, and for as long as you're in my arms, you're safe."

Vaughn gasped and kissed him again with an eagerness bordering on despair.

Finley rolled them gently on the bed. He was still hard inside Vaughn. He rested his forearms left and right of Vaughn's head and played with his red curls. Rolling his hips, he slowly, carefully, made love to his overwhelmed-looking mate. "You're stunning like this."

"Like what?" Vaughn whispered. "Helpless and weak?"

Finley kissed the dumb words away. "No. Open. Believe me, there's nothing weak about sharing your fears with your man." He peppered Vaughn's face with kisses. Finley moaned at the exquisite pressure of Vaughn's channel around his shaft. "Fuck, you feel like home." He shuddered. "Smell like home, too."

Vaughn brought his hands up and slid them over Finley's chest then up to his shoulders. He traced the faint scars on Finley's upper arms. Rolling up from the bed, he started kissing and licking them.

Finley hissed. "I need more."

"Take what you need." Vaughn squeezed his muscles rhythmically around Finley's cock and made his balls pull tight. Vaughn's prick was once again hard, hot, and leaking against Finley's belly. Obviously, the slow pace was killing them both.

However, Finley loved the passion of their coupling. "No.

You will take what *you* need. You know how much I want you. Show me you want me as well."

Vaughn growled. "Bastard."

"We need to work on your endearments, hun." Finley snapped his hips, hitting Vaughn's prostate.

The man threw back his head and yelled. "Fuck! Yes, oh God!"

Finley would never get enough of this. He'd always loved sex, but seeing Vaughn writhing underneath him beat everything he'd ever experienced. He kept up with the slow, deep strokes until Vaughn's grip on his arms tightened and Vaughn shot all over his belly.

A couple of quick thrusts later, Finley followed his mate into orgasmic bliss. He couldn't remember the last time he'd come so hard. Finley carefully slid out of Vaughn and rolled to his back, taking Vaughn with him until his mate nestled against his side. They were both panting for breath.

"Wow." Finley trailed his fingers up and down Vaughn's back. His pale damp skin glistened in the dim morning light shining through the thin curtains. Finley noticed a smattering of freckles on Vaughn's shoulder and vowed to tease them with his tongue someday.

Vaughn's breath fanned over his chest and left nipple, teasing the nub to a permanent peak. From time to time he'd rub his nose over Finley's skin and kiss his pectoral. Vaughn ran his fingers over the ridges of Finley's chest then down his side. A deep sigh expanded his chest. A thick blanket of silence hung between them.

Finley kissed Vaughn's hair.

"I killed my mate."

Those words fell into the quiet between them like rocks into a calm, clear lake. Finley closed his eyes but didn't stop caressing Vaughn's back.

"Why aren't you saying anything?"

"I'm waiting for you to tell me how you think you caused his death."

Vaughn snorted and sat up, showing Fin his back. "So you can tell me I'm wrong and to get over it?"

"No. I wish to understand you." Finley would never be so insensitive as to tell his mate his feelings weren't valid.

Vaughn looped his arms around his knees. "I met Walter when he joined the pack. He was thirty-five and I was eighteen. For me that was a huge gap. I looked up to him, worshiped him because he was so mature, so knowledgeable. A real doctor with a degree. I was the bastard son of a low-level enforcer, a troublemaker who liked to fight with other boys. The former alpha, Don's mother, encouraged such behavior. Walter took me under his wing. I became his assistant, and he trained me as a nurse."

"Sounds as though he was good for you." Finley smiled. He didn't have a reason to feel jealous or threatened.

"For a while." Vaughn stared straight ahead. He moved his toes under the sheet, obviously curling and uncurling them. "Walter was a pacifist. He hated my dedication to my status as a fighter for the pack. He'd have preferred me to stay in the infirmary with him full time. That wasn't me." He laughed, but it wasn't a happy sound. "Maybe you'll think I was a bad mate to him. We learn from a young age that a mate completes you and wants to please you. That you'll do anything to please your mate." Vaughn ran a hand through his hair and looked over his shoulder. "I couldn't. I didn't. As I got older, I longed to spread my wings."

Finley sat up on his knees and moved closer, placed his arms around Vaughn's shoulders from behind and leaned against his back. "Mating is never roses and rainbows. My parents always said every relationship requires work. Compromises. Conversations."

"True. Walter's and my conversations were usually pretty

heated. He wanted us to have kids. I didn't. I wanted to go out with him on occasion, he didn't. He thought our pack shouldn't engage with your neighboring pride, I did."

Finley slid his palms around Vaughn and over his pectorals. "I'm sorry you had problems. But surely you loved each other very much. It's in your voice whenever you mention him."

"Yeah." Vaughn sniffed. "That's what made our fights more painful. I'm not an easy guy, as you've painfully learned over the past few weeks. I'm stubborn, and I tend to run when emotions are involved. Walter must've been frustrated as hell." He rubbed the back of his hand under his nose.

Finley kissed Vaughn's nape. "What happened?"

"We had one last fight. Walter had found a surrogate without discussing it with me. I told him I wasn't ready for kids, and he accused me of stalling on purpose until he was too old for them. I was mad because he'd seen right through me." A shiver ran through Vaughn's body. His skin, still damp from their romp, felt chilly, so Finley placed a blanket around his shoulders and cuddled against his back.

"Parenthood is always a hard topic for both parties, because there's no compromise," Finley said quietly.

"I yelled at him. Accused him of using our future baby to tie me down, keep me from doing my job as a fighter." Vaughn sniffed again. "I was horrible to him. He looked so crestfallen. Heartbroken." He placed his hands over his face, his shoulders shaking. "I told him I was going out and not to wait up for me. Drove to the nearest bar and got rip-roaring drunk. Walter and Beta Raul kept calling my cell, but I ignored them both. I'd totally forgotten I was scheduled for patrol duty." Vaughn broke out in sobs and fell back against Finley's chest.

Finley carefully lowered Vaughn's body back onto the mattress. Vaughn curled into a fetal position, with his head on

Finley's legs and his arms slung around Fin's waist.

"He took my shift. The dumbass pacifist took my shift, and he was shot by poachers. Died instantly." Vaughn let out a wail. "And the last words I said to him were full of anger."

"Oh, baby." Finley blanketed Vaughn's body with his own, stroking and caressing him anywhere he could reach. His own tears fell, but he didn't stop peppering Vaughn's skin with kisses. "I'm so sorry."

Vaughn's fingers clutched Fin's arms. "Do you understand? You're an enforcer. You accompany me on stupid, dangerous missions. I can't trust you to stay safe, Finley. If something were to happen to you . . . I can't lose another mate." He sat up and brushed his hands over his red-rimmed eyes. "I'm on the edge. If we mate and you die, it'll gut me and I'll take a flying leap. That's why I avoided talking to you. That's why I didn't want to be friends. I'm scared shitless."

Finley sat silently for a moment, choosing his next words carefully. He didn't want to offend his grieving mate. "Vaughn, considering your earlier reaction when you thought the assassin had shot me, I'd say a mate mark won't make a difference in the end. You care about me, or you wouldn't have flipped. Hell, you wouldn't be in my bed. With or without the bite wound on our necks, I can't live without you."

Vaughn's gaze snapped up to meet his. "You don't know me."

"My cougar knows who you are to us. My cat and I . . . we love you."

Vaughn's eyes widened. "I don't . . . I'm not sure—"

Fin placed his fingers over Vaughn's lips. "Shh. It's fine." Taking a deep breath, Fin reached up and took off his tags. He slowly slid them over Vaughn's head, touching them where they come to rest in the middle of his chest. "No matter how long it takes, I'll wait for the day your heart and my love find each other."

"Oh God." Vaughn's next kiss took him by surprise and felt like an attack. The man's lips tasted salty. His face was hot under Finley's fingers. "You're too good for me."

"Am not. Please stop pushing me away. We can shelve the emotional stuff until we're back with the pride, if you prefer. But you need to accept that I'll fight for us." Finley looked into Vaughn's eyes. "And never again suggest I shouldn't fight by your side. You didn't want Walter to cut your freedom for the sake of your safety. Don't try the same with me."

Vaughn squeezed his eyes closed. "Fuck. You're right."

"We're a team. We'll have each other's backs." Fin pressed a kiss between Vaughn's unruly curls. "Give us a chance."

"I should've known. Cats are too damn stubborn."

CHAPTER SIX

Vaughn turned the car into the parking lot at the Eagle Mountain Trailhead deep in Superior National Forest. They'd left Minneapolis early in the morning, headed toward Duluth. From there they'd followed the road along the north shore of Lake Superior. The scenery was beautiful. Crystal-clear blue water glittered with a blinding intensity. High, slender conifers in a lush and healthy green hue grew toward the sky and spread close to the shore. The air was crisp and clear.

"The forest covers about four million acres," Finley said as he absently slid his finger over one of the maps Bailey had given them. "That's amazing. My cougar wants us to shift and explore." He laughed. "Eagle Mountain's the highest point in Minnesota, and it's only a three-and-a-half-mile hike away. According to Bailey's map, we need to circle the mountain and go on until we reach Goose Lake, where the lab's located." Finley looked up and frowned. "Why didn't we hide the car somewhere? We'll need to buy a permit from the kiosk if we start our hike from the trailhead."

"It's called *blending in*. I changed our license plates to ones from Minnesota before we left the hotel this morning." Vaughn opened the middle console and retrieved two wallets. "We'll play a couple going on a camping trip. Perfectly normal and unsuspicious, even this time of the year. The area is crawling with forest rangers. If one of them finds our SUV hidden in the woods, we'll be in trouble." He handed Finley one of the wallets. "Fake IDs. We're Joe and Mike Summers.

We're from Alexandria, Minnesota, and we've been married for three years. Happy anniversary, stalker." Vaughn climbed out of the SUV and stretched. He groaned when his tendons popped. He wasn't ashamed to admit, at least to himself, that the prospect of leading Finley into a potentially dangerous situation didn't sit right with him. But he'd promised Finley not to treat him like a child.

Their night together had changed Vaughn's life irrevocably, and although his coyote was content, Vaughn's head almost exploded with hundreds of possible *what ifs*. To distract himself, he opened the trunk and discreetly checked the guns and knives he'd stashed in his backpack yesterday. Vaughn carried another gun and two knives hidden under his clothes.

Finley slid from the car and joined him at the back of the car. "I love hiking. And these woods are lovely. I haven't been on a hiking trip in years, I think. I used to be jealous of Tony's brother Viggo. He's a rock climbing and hiking guide and used to travel for extended periods for his job."

"Viggo's the European Wildcat?" Vaughn lifted his backpack out of the trunk and slid it onto his back.

Finley nodded. "He hasn't left the village since he met his mate, Jax. I bet he's getting twitchy. You investigated the pride, huh?" Fin shouldered his own backpack and looked around. "Let's buy our permits."

Vaughn followed Finley to the tiny kiosk and let his mate deal with the chipper clerk who explained the obstacles of a wilderness trail and that they'd better look where they set their feet because cell phone coverage was non-existent and help wasn't easy to find in case of an emergency. Finley nodded patiently and engaged in a light and flirty chitchat with the friendly guy.

Vaughn barely suppressed a growl. "Let's go, honey. We have quite a distance to hike today." He tugged at Finley's flannel shirt.

Finley bid the clerk goodbye and followed Vaughn out of the kiosk. "No need to be jealous, *Mike*."

"Are you always this friendly to strangers?" Vaughn stomped across the parking area toward the start of the trail. As soon as the trees closed around them, the air was chillier and slightly damp. The scents of humus and various critters hit his twitching nose. Vaughn had denied his coyote a run for too long, and now the animal wanted to run freely. *Patience, boy.*

Finley laughed. He obviously had no trouble keeping up with Vaughn's brisk steps. "Yes. Being friendly costs nothing, and it puts your counterpart at ease. People also tend to remember you in more detail when you were unfriendly to them."

"I know how to talk with people. I'm a private eye," he snapped.

Finley clapped him on the shoulder. "Relax. I'm completely and irrevocably yours. But let's concentrate on the mission." He looked over his shoulder and lowered his voice. "Xander wants us to snoop around but said to stay out of the lab if possible."

"That's nonsense. We'll learn next to nothing from peering over the fence with our binoculars." Vaughn shook his head. "I get your alpha's worries, but if he wants solid information to plan a successful attack, he'll need more than the plans Bailey sketched from memory alone. Donavan would tell us to break in and make the most of it."

"I agree. You're a professional, and I'm an ex-soldier. We'll find a way in and out without being seen. And if we're seen . . ." He placed his hand against his side where he carried a gun under his jacket.

Vaughn nodded, returning his focus to the unsteady ground. He jumped over a couple of rocks and roots. Taking a deep breath, Vaughn felt his muscles relax slightly. His coyote was anxious, but the scents of nature around them calmed the beast. Finley must've felt the same, because he snickered behind him.

"The past couple of months haven't been easy," Fin muttered. "First that asshole Hector kidnaps Xander. Then Jaxon was shot during a rescue mission, and we imprisoned a bunch of Hector's fellow deer. Next we're attacked by a squad of crazy killer vamps, one of whom now works for us." Finley sighed deeply. "We used to worry about how to get jobs to keep us fed. About how our kids would get an education good enough so they could attend college. Life used to be so much easier."

Vaughn turned and took the map from Finley's fingers. "As soon as Thoreau's brought down, your life will return to boring and predictable." He studied the map.

"I doubt it." Fin snorted. "I've got you now. Living with a private investigator slash fighter will never be boring or predictable."

Vaughn chose to ignore the comment. "We have to leave the trail in half a mile. We'll be faster that way."

Nodding, Finley pulled a compass out of his pocket. "Want me to navigate?"

"Do you remember how to do it?" Vaughn teased. He ducked when Fin swiped at him. "All right. Hey, what was your rank anyway?"

"Sergeant First Class." Finley snatched the map back with a glare. "Keep up the cheekiness and I'll sleep in the tent alone, Private." He walked around Vaughn and stalked off with a delicious sway to his hips that should've looked ridiculous on a man of Finley's height and strength.

Vaughn followed, his gaze fixed on Fin's perfectly round butt, and quickly stumbled over a root. He caught himself and blushed when Fin looked over his shoulder. "That root snuck up on me."

"Yeah. Right." Finley left the trail at the mentioned spot and ventured into the thick foliage. They had to slow down considerably because of the terrain. "Let's hope no rangers are around. It should be dark by the time we find the compound."

"Just as planned." Vaughn pushed past some spruce branches Finley held for him. "Thanks. We'll set up base and take a first look around. It won't matter if it's night or day anyway, if shifter guards patrol the area."

Finley checked the map and the compass and adjusted their direction slightly. "True. I bet most of the shifters are of the flying variety, too. We need to be wary of sneaky birds."

"I never thought bird shifters would ever try for world domination. In movies and books, it's always wolves or cats or other large predators." Vaughn retrieved a bottle of water from his backpack and took a couple of sips. He handed the bottle to Finley when the man held out his hand.

"True." Finley gulped the water. "I admit I'm oblivious when it comes to shifter politics. As an enforcer, I do as Xander says, dumb as that sounds." He screwed the bottle closed and gave it back to Vaughn.

Vaughn shrugged. "It's your job, just like it was mine. I've been living in Sioux Falls for a year since I left the pack, though. I've worked as security for a couple of shifter kids. And you wouldn't believe how many councilmen hire PIs."

"To spy on their spouses?"

"Sometimes. But mostly to spy on other councilmen. People—some of them clients—have gone missing over the past few months. That's why I was investigating the whole lot when Donavan contacted me. I warned him to stay out of this mess. I had no idea he was already neck-deep."

"Tell me what you know."

Vaughn's nose twitched as he caught a scent. He looked up and quickly grabbed Finley's arm, halting him. "Shh. Quiet. Don't move." Fifty feet in front of them, a medium-sized gray wolf emerged from a row of thick shrubs. Finley tensed beside him when the animal fixed them with its yellow-brown eyes. The wolf was beautiful in its sleek strength. It growled at them, showing its teeth, but didn't come closer.

Vaughn's coyote wasn't amused. In his shifted form, he'd be smaller and leaner than the wolf. And Vaughn wasn't looking forward to hurting an animal trying to protect its territory. But he would if the wolf turned out to be a danger to Finley.

Finley laughed. "I'll deal with him." A deep, rumbling growl built in the man's chest, becoming louder and louder until it was a vicious snarl that rose the hair on Vaughn's nape. His coyote cowered and whined inside his head. *Fuck, my man is strong.*

The wolf obviously thought so, too. It whined and shuffled around, tucking its tail. When Finley snarled again, the wolf yipped, turned, and ran off.

"See. That won't help us if he comes back with the whole pack in tow, but we got rid of him." Finley grinned. "No reason to draw your gun."

"Thanks. I'd have shifted. Don't honestly think I'd pull the trigger on an innocent animal looking so much like my own." Vaughn swallowed the bile rising in his throat. He brushed the back of his hand over his damp forehead.

Finley's eyes widened. "Shit! I'm so sorry. I didn't mean—"

"It's fine. You didn't remember." He nudged Fin. "Let's go before he comes back and hope we don't meet a bear next." They continued for five minutes until Vaughn remembered what they'd been discussing. "Donavan had me investigating Councilman Eric Tinsel. He's one of three coyote representatives on the Council. Tinsel suggested Donavan should stay out of Xander's dispute with Thoreau. I found out Tinsel owes money to some seriously bad guys in Sioux Falls. He's a gambling addict. Was close to losing his house to the bank and his wife to someone else because he had to sell her jewelry. Two months ago he receives a huge payment from an off-shore bank account, and his debts of approximately one million dollars are gone. Vanished."

Finley whistled. "Thoreau?"

"I'm sure of it. Why else would a coyote shifter vote against his own people in a dispute over land between a flock of eagles and a coyote pack in Wisconsin not two weeks later?"

"Fuck." Finley let out a deep breath. "What else?"

Vaughn adjusted his backpack. "Many of the avian councilmen receive money from the same bank account as Tinsel. Others face harassment by threatening Emails and letters. They're concerned about the safety of their families, so they're reluctant to vote Thoreau out of office."

"It's just a matter of time until Thoreau introduces a law that makes it impossible to vote against him." Finley shook his head. "That's what dictators do to ensure their reign continues. Why would he want to rule alone? Sounds like too much hassle to me. Is it money? Power?"

Vaughn climbed over a fallen log. "Both, I guess. He was a power-hungry control freak as a councilman, before he became president. However, everyone was surprised when he decided to run for the office."

"Why?" Finley frowned.

"Rumor had it he wanted to retire from politics altogether. Apparently, he was frustrated with the constant debates that typically led nowhere. He was among those who thought one councilman per species is enough because the more members the slower the decision process."

Finley pressed his lips into a flat line. "He's not completely wrong. The seats per species should be restricted. We need a better voting system, too. Some packs and prides live so far from civilization they can't vote. Some species aren't represented at all. That's not right."

"I agree. I had a chat with Armand. They have a completely

different system in Europe."

Finley stopped and met his gaze. "Maybe that's why Armand relinquished his position in Europe and came to the US."

Finley had wondered how it was possible to hide a secret lab and training facility for altered humans in the middle of a national forest without anyone being the wiser. Obviously, the people in charge had thought about that as well and had changed some things since Bailey had been stationed there.

The sprawling complex he and Vaughn were looking at from their hiding spot resembled the base of a logging company. Trucks—some empty, some loaded with massive logs and ready to leave through the huge main gate—filled the lot. The complex was bigger than Bailey's hand-drawn map had indicated. It was also flooded with light, thanks to the many spotlights placed methodically throughout the area.

"Shit," Vaughn muttered beside him. He held his binoculars pressed to his face. "We need an exceptional entry plan. Have you seen how many people are down there? And they've built new buildings. Maybe they relocated the lab."

"We're fucked. But I have to admit a logging company is a good cover."

Vaughn growled and looked at him. "Keep on praising our enemies and you'll be the one sleeping outside tonight."

Smirking, Finley looked through his own binoculars. He followed the paths from one building to the next, taking in every detail and filing them for later use. "The original buildings have heavier surveillance. And steel doors. I doubt they relocated the lab." He hummed. "Looks like they became wary of the human authorities and built the logging company around the old complex. Makes sense in case of an inspection by humans."

Vaughn grunted. "I see a fancy sign on the assumed lab building. *Superior Flooring.*"

Finley lifted the binoculars from his eyes and rolled onto his back. He looked up at the canopy of trees. Then he snapped his fingers. "Flooring. Of course. You need a palette of chemicals and a testing lab to turn wood flakes to laminate. Damn, they're clever."

"Fucking hell." Vaughn reached out and placed one arm over Finley's chest, wriggling closer until they lay pressed together from shoulder to feet. "According to Bailey's files, the labs are underground. I bet they have a clean lab on the ground floor as cover."

Finley racked his brain. "The increased manpower might work to our advantage. We're less likely to attract attention among those flannel-clad woodworkers and truck drivers." He shivered and snuggled closer against Vaughn. Fin would love to shift. The ground was chilly through the mats they'd placed under their bodies, and the cold seeped through his protective gear. His furry form would be much better suited to withstand the cold.

"Yeah. We need a way to reach the inner area. A second fence separates it from the busy parts of the complex." Vaughn turned his face and pressed a kiss against his temple, nuzzling him for a moment. "You take a nap in the tent and warm up. I'll keep watch and take notes about shift changes, guard rotation, and anything else I see from our perch."

Finley didn't want to leave Vaughn alone. Sure, they had walkie talkies, but they'd erected the tent deep in the woods, five human walking minutes from the stakeout place. If Vaughn was in trouble, it'd take Finley as least two minutes in his shifted form to reach his mate. However, they had to cover a whole twenty-four hours of watching the compound if they wanted a chance to sneak inside. If they missed something, things could go terribly wrong.

Sighing deeply, Finley kissed his mate's cheek. "You can take the first six hours, but I'm not leaving you. I'll shift and take a nap. My cougar has fantastic ears. He'll notice every little threat that tries to sneak up on us." He met Vaughn's deep green eyes.

Vaughn huffed. "I've staked out places before. I won't go down there with guns blazing as soon as you turn your back."

"You better not, or I'll spank you until you can't sit for a whole week." Finley ignored Vaughn's incredulous expression and gave him another quick kiss. Since they'd had sex, Finley felt more attuned to Vaughn's conflicted feelings and mood swings. The vibes he caught from his mate alarmed him. A certain recklessness and desperation brewed deep inside Vaughn that made for an explosive mixture.

Fin sat up and peeled out of his clothes. As soon as he was down to his undershirt he started shivering. "Stop glaring while I undress." He laughed. "I'd rather you heat me up with a smoldering look."

Vaughn rolled his eyes, but a small smile graced his lips. "Hurry up, furball, before you freeze your balls off. I've got plans for those."

As soon as Fin was naked, he initiated his shift. Being an enforcer, he didn't take long to arrive at his cougar form. Finley raised his butt in the air and stretched extensively in true cat fashion. He yawned and licked his muzzle.

Vaughn chuckled beside him. Reaching out, Vaughn placed his hand on his shoulder. "Wow. Your fur is way softer than I imagined." He slid his hand up and scratched behind Finley's ear. "Purr for me."

Fin squeezed his eyes shut. His cat loved a good scratch. And a petting from his mate . . . pure bliss. He pushed into the caress, purring up a storm. Finley licked his mate's cheek and huddled closer.

Vaughn grimaced, rubbing his hand down his face. "Gah.

Cougar slobber." He touched his index finger to Fin's soft nose. "Rascal. If you insist on staying, at least make yourself useful and keep me warm." He rolled back to his front and raised his binoculars.

Finley chuffed. He climbed across his mate and flopped down over his ass and thighs. He started grooming his paws and face. With Vaughn's acceptance of their protection, his cat was happy as a clam.

Vaughn had obviously lived in a state of complete disregard for his own safety since Walter had passed away. To some extent, Finley understood where Vaughn was coming from. Most shifters didn't live long after they lost their fated mate. The animals inside them pined away and eventually died of a broken heart. And it wasn't often fate granted a second mate. But being on a mission with a man whose mental stability resembled a powder keg about to go off put Finley in a difficult situation.

Finley had come inside Vaughn last night. And he'd tasted some of his blood during a passionate, frenzied kiss. The bonding process had started. And if Vaughn put himself in danger because he thought he had nothing to live for without Walter in his life, Fin wasn't sure whether he had the power to save the man he loved.

CHAPTER SEVEN

Two days of watching the compound passed before Vaughn and Finley felt they had sufficient knowledge to infiltrate the operation without sticking out like sore thumbs.

Shielded by the dark of the night, Vaughn followed Finley through the forest because the cougar had better night vision. That was the sole reason he'd allowed Finley, after a heavy argument, to lead the mission. On the outside they looked like the other lumberjacks Vaughn had seen enter and leave on a daily basis, but underneath they both wore bulletproof vests.

Vaughn clutched his thermos tighter when Finley stopped at the tree line and waited for him. As soon as they left the forest, there'd be no going back. They knew how many shifters and vamps patrolled the grounds, how many people were on each shift, and how often they changed. They'd taken pictures of every vehicle and person who entered or left the facility. Finley had made a list of the guns the personnel were packing.

Finley was hell-bent on sneaking inside the lab building to take pictures of the security measures and to look for captive shifters. Based on Bailey's insider intel, Taylor used the blood of captured shifters to turn his human volunteers into bloodthirsty assassins, but they had no idea if the shifters were on site.

Vaughn knew chances were high they'd encounter one or more vamps at the lab.

Finley carried a white plastic box with a green lid for appearances sake. Hopefully they'd pass for two guys who'd spent their lunch break outside. Earlier they'd packed up their tent, clothes, and other equipment, and stowed everything in the bed of a sturdy pickup truck parked in the employees' parking area outside of the compound. They'd learned, from watching the gates, that the owner had started a twelve-hour guard shift. Thankfully, the parking lot itself had been blessedly unguarded.

"Ready?" Finley asked.

"As I'll ever be." Vaughn checked the various guns he carried hidden under his clothes one last time, then nodded. "Go."

Finley left the forest and strolled toward the back entrance of the compound as though he had every right to. He laughed and bumped against Vaughn's shoulder as soon as Vaughn caught up to him. "You still owe me fifty, man," he said loudly as they came closer to the open double door manned by a single security guard. Earlier that day, Fin had seen the guard being led around and introduced to others by a superior. He was obviously new on the team and wouldn't know everyone on staff. Their perfect chance.

"Fifty? In your dreams," Vaughn muttered.

"I told you the Panthers had no chance against the Redskins. You should've seen Alan's face when his team failed." Fin laughed.

Vaughn frowned, trying to catch up with Finley's words. He understood the need for diversion. He wasn't dumb. But hell, he had no idea what Fin was babbling about aside from remembering both teams played football. "Yeah, I never should've accepted the bet. You can't trust Alan's tips." It probably didn't hurt their role-play that he didn't sound enthusiastic, seeing as he'd obviously lost money.

Finley nodded at the security guard, who had an ID clipped to his breast pocket. Vaughn saw the handgun strapped to the man's hip and detected another hidden under his pants leg. The strap of his machine gun was slung over his shoulder.

The guard frowned. "What were you two doing outside?" He shifted nervously from one foot to the other.

Finley smirked. "We took a break. A guy needs to eat."

"You can do that inside. We have a canteen." The guard — Frank according to his name tag — looked at them, a suspicious gleam in his eyes. His gaze fell on the fake ID dangling on a lanyard around Vaughn's neck.

Vaughn kept his face passive. He'd designed the IDs based on one of the high-resolution pictures Finley had taken during the day shift and hoped he'd gotten close enough to the real thing. But if the guard checked too thoroughly, he'd recognize them as fake.

Finley laughed and slapped Vaughn's belly with the back of his hand. "Told you he'd ask us. Frank's new. Look." Fin lowered his voice and leaned toward Frank. "My buddy and I wanted some privacy for our break." When the guard frowned harder, Finley smirked. "You understand? Can't have Mike here sucking me off in the restroom of the canteen. What if the other guys found out?"

Frank's eyes widened in horror. Next his face twisted into a mask of disgust. "You're fags? God. Get back to work. If I ever hear you've been fucking around on company time, I'll tell my boss. Fucking gross." He shuddered, backed away from them, and waved his hand impatiently.

Finley winked at him, but Vaughn grabbed his arm and forced him to hurry up. "What the hell? Trying to have us killed?"

"It worked. Bigots usually don't want to come closer to gays. Not even to check IDs." Fin smiled as he looked around. "And maybe I was trying to give you a hint. Two days, and you haven't touched me."

"We're on a mission," Vaughn hissed. "Keep your mind

out of my pants." He glanced around, but none of the other men around them paid any attention. They were blending in perfectly, as many men carried a lunch box and thermos. Perfect timing.

Finley rolled his eyes and murmured, "Relax. They'll see you're as tense as a bowstring. We're lumberjacks on a break. You look like a US spy sneaking through the guts of the Kremlin. I know you've done this before. You were cool as a cucumber when you led Romeo inside the Council prison."

"Well, I lost my coolness once I started worrying about your safety." As soon as the words had left his mouth, Vaughn wished he had the chance to take them back. He'd been the one who banned private conversations involving emotions during dangerous situations, and here he was bringing it up himself.

Thank God Finley merely slapped his back briefly and trudged on. "Over there." He dipped his head toward the trucks parked beside the fence separating the inner from the outer area. They hoped the huge vehicles parked beside the fence provided enough cover to cut a hole in the mesh wire. On the other side of the fence, a big gas tank gave them shelter from the security cameras.

Vaughn casually strode to the truck closest to the fence and slipped behind it. He knelt down and lifted his hand. Finley opened the lunch box and dropped a small wire cutter into his open palm.

"Enjoy your lunch, babe."

Vaughn chuckled quietly as he made quick work of the wire, creating a hole big enough for them to squeeze through. Sneaking another peek around, Vaughn carefully climbed through. He held the mesh while Finley followed. Ducking low, they snuck around the gas tank and stopped in its shade.

"We need lab coats or something as soon as we're inside," Finley whispered.

Vaughn focused on the surveillance cameras. "*If* we get inside. Let's hope Bailey's code still works. Come on." Thank God the area was full of stacked crates filled with lab supplies. In the relative darkness, it was easy to run from one crate to the next and hide from the cameras. But eventually they ran out of cover and had to sprint the last twenty feet separating them from a side entrance before the rotating camera caught them.

Vaughn let Finley go first and followed the man quickly over dried grass and dusty earth, their combat boots barely making a sound. They huddled by the door, Vaughn shielding Fin's back with his body. Finley reached to press the numbers on the keypad beside the door when it swung open abruptly and a young man wearing a green lab coat stepped out. The guy froze when he saw them, a cigarette dangling from between his lips. He held a lighter in one hand and the door with the other.

Reacting quickly, Finley punched the guy in the face. The slight man let out a muffled sound and crumbled. While Fin caught him, Vaughn held the door wide. "Hurry." Vaughn shot a quick look over his shoulder.

Fin dragged the guy inside the building. "He's human."

"Fuck." Vaughn helped Fin peel the man out of his lab coat. Looking up, he noticed a door labeled *Cleaning Supplies.* "Get dressed. I'll take care of our friend." Vaughn grabbed the man's wrists and quickly slid him over the gleaming tile floor. He pushed the door open to find a small, closet-like room stuffed with shelves holding buckets and canisters of chemicals. He leaned the man against one of the shelves and zip-tied his wrists and ankles. Taking off his bandana, he gagged the guy. Last, he affixed the man's bound wrists to the shelf and took his lanyard.

When Vaughn left the room and closed the door quietly behind him, he found Fin waiting for him, dressed in the green coat. He looked at the photo on the lanyard before he handed it to Fin. "At least the dude has brown hair, too."

Fin placed the lanyard around his neck and shrugged. "Let's go find another coat for you."

"Yeah. And an elevator. We need to head downstairs. I doubt we'll find anything up here." Vaughn checked out the security measures as he followed Finley along the stark white corridor. His coyote was agitated. He hated the scent of anti-septic and bleach that hung heavy in the air, because it made smelling other people next to impossible.

Finley closed his fingers around his wrist and tugged him to the left. "Elevator," he said and pointed upward at a sign. They reached the promised elevator after twenty feet. Finley pushed the button impatiently. "How will we explain your presence?"

Vaughn shrugged. "We don't. Let's stick with the *punching their lights out* strategy for now."

"Cool." Fin bounced his left leg, looking up at the numbers on the panel. As soon as the elevator doors slid open, Finley rushed inside. "Damn." He pointed at the box attached beside the buttons for the different floors. "Of course, access is re-stricted."

"Try the guy's ID."

Finley held the stolen lanyard against the box, letting out a puff of air when the light turned green and the doors closed. "Floor?"

"According to Bailey, the interesting stuff is all the way down."

Fin pressed the button for the lowest floor.

Vaughn checked his weapons. "No assassins so far. I mean, it *is* late at night, but the whole place is eerily quiet." A surprising contrast to the bustling activity outside. He craned his neck until the tense tendons popped. "I don't like this."

"I reckon evil scientists need their beauty sleep, too." The elevator dinged and the doors opened, revealing yet another white corridor. "Haven't these guys heard of the concept of color?" Fin whispered as he peered down the corridor. "This white freaks me out. It's a cross between a hospital and a slaughterhouse."

Vaughn drew his semi-automatic and leaned out of the elevator. "Considering what's going on down here, you're not so far off. Let's go." Vaughn noticed the security cameras right away. "CCTV every sixty feet." A seemingly endless row of steel doors stretched left and right of the corridor. Beside every door, Vaughn saw the same access boxes as those in the elevator. The floors were squeaky clean. "We need to act as normal as possible. As though we belong."

"Maybe you should wait for me. As soon as we leave the elevator, whoever's manning the camera room will see you're an intruder." Finley touched his arm. "I'll be careful."

"Forget it." Vaughn pointed at the steel door closest to them, then placed his hand against the elevator door to keep it from sliding closed. "Go and open it. I'll follow as soon as you have access."

From the pinch of his lips, Finley didn't look happy, but he nodded anyway and strode briskly to the door. "The sign has a number, no description." He swiped the card over the reader and winced when the box let out an angry beep.

"What is it?" Vaughn tightened his hold on his gun.

"Damn light's blinking red. That doesn't look good. The guy from upstairs obviously isn't allowed to play with the big boys."

"Shit."

Finley tried scanning the ID again with the same result. "How are we—"

The door to Fin's right opened. Out stepped a tall, slim man with white-blond hair in a blue lab coat. He squinted when his gaze fell on Finley. "What do you think you're doing? You don't have access to that area." The man hadn't seen Vaughn hidden in the elevator yet. He swiftly walked toward Finley, a haughty expression on his lean face.

When the man walked past the elevator, Vaughn detected the faint smell of avian shifter.

"Uh . . ." Finley waved his ID card. "My boss told me to—"

The stranger's eyes narrowed. "Bullshit." He snatched the lanyard out of Finley's fingers and held it up. "Prentiss Clark. Hm. Yeah, looks exactly like you. I'll call security." He slid his hand into his lab coat.

Vaughn soundlessly left the elevator and came up behind the stranger. He pointed his gun right at the back of the guy's head. "Raise your hands. Slowly."

The man whirled around. His eyes widened, and his mouth clapped open in shock. "How dare you—"

Vaughn pointed the muzzle of his gun at the man's forehead until he got the message and lifted his hands. "He's secured. Try his ID, babe." He growled. "Don't move, asshole, or I'll put a bullet between your eyes."

The stranger's pale blue eyes blazed with hatred. "Do you have any idea who I am?"

Finley yanked the lanyard from the guy's neck and read, *"Doctor Zane Taylor. Head of Research and Development."*

Holy shit. *The* Doctor Taylor?

Finley met the doctor's gaze, a cold smile on his face. "Nice to finally meet you, Doc. I've heard stories about you. None of them good." He swiped the card over the reader. The light switched to green, and the steel door snicked open. Fin pushed it wide. "Bring the Doc, honey."

Taylor growled. "You're making a stupid mistake. It'll be your last. You won't get out of the lab alive."

Vaughn slammed the butt of his gun against Taylor's temple and watched in satisfaction as the guy stumbled. While

Taylor cradled his head, Vaughn grabbed a fistful of Taylor's lab coat and pushed him through the door. "Shut the fuck up, Frankenstein. We should kill you for your crazy experiments. Altering sick humans so they turn into blood-sucking killer machines." Vaughn quickly closed the door behind them.

"Security will be here soon. At least one guard mans the camera room at all times." Taylor glared. But when Vaughn pointed his gun at him again, his face paled and he huddled against the wall. It was obvious from his cowering posture he was a scientist without one fighting bone in his body. "Wait wait *wait*! You're a shifter too. Who cares about those stupid humans? They'd die without my cure anyway. They're monsters who only serve one purpose."

"Yeah. To kill for Thoreau." Fin spat. He drew his own gun and pointed it at the doc. "Take off your coat. My friend needs it."

With only one nudge of Fin's gun, Taylor quickly slid out of the garment and threw it at Vaughn. "The killer thing was a fortunate side effect. You don't know what you're getting yourself into." Taylor's nostrils flared. "Did you come to take down our lab? Two poorly-equipped wanna-be soldiers?" He laughed. "It's not the first time some crazy human rights extremists broke in to free our subjects. I give you ten minutes before you're dead."

Vaughn shrugged the coat on. "Hey, babe. We can't risk taking him with us, although I'd love to give the boss a chance to question him. Let's leave Thoreau a message through the good doctor instead." He grinned when Taylor paled even more. Sweat glistened on his skin. "I hear you take it up the ass from our dear president. How would he like to find his poor mate sliced to ribbons as a warning?"

"How did you . . ." Taylor trailed off. A shudder worked through his body. "If you hurt me, he'll retaliate."

Fin raked the muzzle of his gun over the blond stubble on

Taylor's chin. "Did he force you to create the assassins because you're his mate? You supply an army of fanged soldiers, and in return he gives you a couple of days a year where he fucks you behind his faithful wife's back?"

"Don't mention that bitch!" Taylor yelled, then snapped his mouth closed. "Do whatever the hell you want with me, but I won't tell you shit. You'll regret you ever got involved in this war. Do you think killing me will stop the revolution?"

"Revolution?" Finley rolled his eyes. He cocked his arm and punched Taylor. The doctor's head slammed back against the wall, and he crumbled to the floor.

"Now, why did you do that?" Vaughn sighed.

"He's an asshole?" Fin shook out his hand. "He wouldn't have told us anything significant. He wanted to keep us talking until the guards arrived. What should we do with him?"

Vaughn pulled out a couple of zip ties. "I only kill to protect myself. And it can't hurt if he tells Thoreau about our visit. Xander wanted us to be stealthy, but this might work to our advantage."

Fin frowned. "They've switched locations before. What if they decide to pack up and leave?"

"Let them." Vaughn smirked. "Moving an operation of this size takes time. Setting up security at a new place takes time. We can plan our attack during the moving process, while they're still on the road. Think about it. This compound is a fortress. But if they decide to move . . . No fences. No cameras. Just guarded trucks hauling a fragmented lab around the country."

"Fine." Finley nodded. "I still want to check out a couple more rooms, please. In case they have shifters down here."

Vaughn grabbed Taylor by the lapels of his checkered suit jacket. "We need to hide this nutjob." He dragged the doctor past a couple of lab tables littered with paperwork filled with formulas and graphs. Vaughn noticed a long desk stretching along the back wall that held a row of computers. Colorful screen savers swirled across the black screens. "Perfect." He leaned Taylor against a cabinet and rushed to the back of the room. Vaughn pulled out one of the office chairs, whirled it around and sat down. Wriggling the mouse, he mentally pumped his fist when the computer woke up.

"Vaughn? What the hell? We need to go." Finley came up behind him and leaned over his shoulder. "It's password protected. We don't have time for this."

Vaughn fished Romeo's flash drive out of his pocket, leaned under the desk, and attached it to the slot at the front of the computer. "Special order from your hacker."

"What?" Fin left his position behind Vaughn and leaned his ass against the desk. "When did you plan to inform me?"

Vaughn raised one eyebrow.

Finley threw up his hands. "Asshole." He scowled. "Does it work?"

Vaughn concentrated on the screen, seeing a window pop up at the upper right corner. Rows of code appeared in the window, scrolling down and down and down until the log-in screen disappeared. "I think so." Vaughn kept his fingers off the keyboard, knowing not to interfere with Romeo's program.

Finley leaned closer to the screen. "Damn." He whistled when random files opened and closed in rapid succession. "Romeo is one smart cookie. His talent is spooky. I'm glad he's on our side. How will we know when the download process is done?"

"I'm sure Thoreau has his own hackers, or he wouldn't have found us." Vaughn scratched his head. "And I have no idea. We wait until the windows stop popping up?" He looked up at Fin.

Finley rolled his eyes. "Great plan. If you had involved me in your side job, I'd have factored it in. We need to work on your communication." He flicked his hand back and forth between them. "You can't keep shit like that from me."

"You're right." Vaughn pushed out of the chair and pressed a quick kiss to Fin's lips. "Forgive me?"

Finley licked his lips. "Only because you're cute." He checked his watch. "Vaughn . . ."

"I know, but—" The computer pinged before it went dark. "What's wrong?"

"What isn't?" Fin reached under the table and unplugged the flash drive. He pocketed it, then held out Taylor's ID. "Guess they found us. Let's go."

Vaughn placed the lanyard around his neck. Leaving the room in a hurry, he urged Fin down the right corridor.

Finley stopped short and stretched his arm across Vaughn's chest. "Someone's coming." He grabbed Vaughn's hand, turned, and ran.

Vaughn stumbled after his mate. "Thank God for cat ears." As they ran from whoever was coming, their soles squeaked on the polished floor, and the heavy thump of their boots echoed in the empty corridor. "Door." At the end of the hallway was a heavy glass escape door. "Stairs."

Finley reached it first and slammed his body against the door. It opened easily enough, but a blaring alarm almost rendered Vaughn deaf. "Shit! Ow." Fin clasped his head, his praised cat ears obviously too sensitive to deal with the noise.

Vaughn pushed Fin up the stairs and turned to look through the closing glass door. Two heavily-armed men in black fatigues came running along the hallway. Relief washed through him when he saw that their eyes and teeth looked normal enough. One of the men raised his gun and fired two shots. Vaughn shouted and fell backward. His back might have painfully hit the stairs if Fin hadn't caught him. Fin slung his arms tightly around Vaughn's chest and tugged at him, panting in Vaughn's ear.

Spider webs spread over the glass where the bullets hit the thankfully bulletproof material. "Fuck. Shit." Vaughn took a shuddering breath and turned in Fin's arms. "Run!"

They hurried upstairs. Big black numbers at the wall on each landing told them how far they had yet to go. When he raced past the first basement landing, Finley let out a curse from above him. The sound of the guards' boots slapping the stairs became louder.

"What?" Vaughn looked up at Finley, who came back down.

"Change of plan. They'll count on us getting out on the ground floor." Finley opened the glass door leading to the first basement. "To the elevator."

Vaughn followed his mate. "Fucking hell. Really? Is that a military move or something?"

"Or something," Fin yelled over the still blaring alarm. "Let's make this more interesting." He came to an abrupt halt, and Vaughn smashed against his back.

"Palmer! Dammit."

Fin pulled the lever for the fire alarm. Vaughn's ears rang as the siren mixed with the other alarm. Scowling at his grinning mate, Vaughn pushed Fin to another steel door, swiped Taylor's card, and pushed Fin into the room. As soon as the heavy door closed behind them, the noise muted to a tolerable level. "I need to take a breath. We don't know what we'll find once we leave the building."

"Probably a couple of thirsty vamps," Fin said as he braced his hands on his hips.

The asshole wasn't out of breath. Vaughn had to up his training. Living in the city and watching politicians from the comfortable safety of his car, had made him soft. Maybe the Frappuccinos and pastries he indulged in on his stakeouts had something to do with it, too. And the cigarettes.

"I need to quit smoking." Vaughn heard raised voices

through the door and the patter of frantic feet. The fire alarm distraction seemed to be working. He took a deep breath and coughed. "What's that smell?"

Finley quickly clamped his hand hard around Vaughn's arm.

"What?" Vaughn took in his mate's wide-eyed expression and shifted his focus. "Holy shit," he gasped.

They'd managed to find the chamber of horrors. The stark white room was tiled from floor to ceiling. In the middle was a morgue-like metal table. Equipment he couldn't name that looked like instruments of torture were stored in high glass cabinets. And in the back of the room were two barred cells.

It became blaringly obvious where the foul smell was coming from. One of the cells held a . . . being . . . that lay on the floor in a twisted, unnatural heap. Sightless, milky eyes stared right at them. The creature's skin was pale and pulled tight over his skull. Long, sharp white teeth were visible in an open mouth.

A shudder ran down Vaughn's back. "Oh my God. So, that's what you end up as when Taylor's cure fails."

"Vaughn," Fin whispered, his voice quivering.

Someone small occupied the other cell. It was hard to tell if the second being was an adult or a child, because the person was wrapped in a blanket and curled up on a ratty cot. The blanket mound shook slightly.

Fin walked over to the cell.

When he reached for the bars, Vaughn pulled him back. "Never touch anything that might be active," he warned. He concentrated on the figure huddled in the corner. "Hey there."

Huge eyes so dark they looked black peeked at him from between the folds of the blanket. A pale, slim hand emerged from the fabric and pulled it tighter. "Please don't hurt me."

The fear ringing in the soft male voice touched Vaughn's

heart.

"We won't hurt you." Finley, bless him, managed a smile for the little one.

Vaughn had to fight not to throw up from the stench in the room. "What's your name?"

Finley snatched the file resting in a holder attached to the wall beside the cell. "Aaron. No last name." He flipped the file open and leafed through it.

Aaron finally uncurled from his position on the cot and stood. Still rolled in the blanket like a burrito, he took two shuffling steps toward the bars. His whole body shook, but Vaughn thought his tremors had more to do with fear — or the dead fellow in the other cell — than the moderate temperature of the room.

"We're the good guys, Aaron," Vaughn said quietly. The fire alarm stopped suddenly. He shot a nervous glance toward the door. It wouldn't be long before the damn guards found them. They had to haul ass. "Fin, can we take him with us?" When he met his mate's worried gaze, Vaughn's stomach dropped. "What?"

Fin's Adam's apple bobbed as he pressed the file to his chest. "They turned him. He's a . . ." Fin peeled his lips away from his teeth and made slurping sounds.

Poor Aaron's eyes widened. "Please!" He rushed forward and curled his skinny fingers around the bars. The blanket slipped off him and revealed a too thin man dressed in a ratty shirt and sweats. "Don't leave me to rot in here. The other guy and I were treated at the same time. See what happened to him?" Aaron let out a sob. "Please let me out."

Vaughn was torn. He bit his bottom lip, taking in Aaron's fragile stature and the huge eyes in his lean face. "Fin, come on. He's no more than a baby vamp. Skin and bones. He can't weigh more than one hundred and twenty pounds soaking wet." Hell, the top of Aaron's head barely reached Vaughn's collarbone.

Fin snorted. "He's probably starving so soon after the change. I'm afraid he'll want to snack on us."

"No!" Aaron shook his head. His long, silver-blond tresses were a tangled mess that reached past his shoulders, down to his waist. "I won't hurt you. You don't have to take me with you. Open the door." Tears filled those round, dark eyes that seemed to look right into Vaughn's soul. "The guys in the lab coats. They swipe their cards over the box whenever they come to take me out for one of their tests. You have the card." He stuck his skinny arm through the bars and reached for Vaughn.

"Shit." Vaughn lifted the lanyard against the box.

"Vaughn! Are you fucking insane?" Fin yelled. He pushed his body between Vaughn and Aaron when the door slid open. He let out a shocked gasp when Aaron launched himself at Fin and threw his arms around Fin's waist with a loud sob.

"Thank you!"

Fin held his hands up in the air, staring down at the blond head nestled against his chest with wide eyes and an open mouth.

"Stop freaking out." Vaughn grabbed the blanket and threw it at Fin. "Wrap him up. We have to go. Now. And don't lose his file. I want Bailey to take a look at it. This doesn't make sense. The kid isn't a fighter. What's the use of little assassins?" He hurried to the door and opened it slowly. Peeking into the hallway, he waved his hand at his companions to speed up. Seconds later, he felt a small body press against his back and heard Finley growl.

"Maybe because they look innocent enough to wrap men around their fingers," Finley muttered.

Vaughn ignored his jealous mate and retrieved his second gun. "Once I step out, I want you two to head to the elevator.

I'll be right behind you and cover you. Fin, make sure Aaron stays between us." When Fin growled again, Vaughn felt Aaron flinch against his back. "Let's go." Vaughn exited the room with both guns raised and pointing down the hallways. He looked left and right, then focused on the left hallway leading away from the elevator. "Okay, come out."

Vaughn heard Finley's heavier boots along with the patter of small, naked feet on the tiles. Damn. Aaron didn't have shoes. Vaughn walked backward, keeping an eye on the hallway and the glass emergency door, trusting Fin to take care of anyone coming at them from the right.

"Twenty feet," Fin said.

Right that moment, three guards pushed through the emergency door. And this time, no glass protected Vaughn. "Run!" He fired both guns, hitting one guard in the chest and another in his right arm. Blood sprayed against the white walls in a cruel arc. The third guard fired at Vaughn, then ducked.

Searing pain hit Vaughn's right hip. He snarled as he was grabbed and dragged. *Fin.* His mate pushed him into the elevator, where Aaron sat huddled on the ground, his arms around his head. Fin took the lanyard, swiped it, and hit the button.

"Where were you hit? I can smell blood."

"Hip." Vaughn handed one of his guns to Fin and pressed his palm against his side. "It's only a graze, but I wonder what part of me he was aiming for. My nuts?"

Fin cursed.

"Hey." Vaughn cupped Fin's nape and pulled their foreheads together. "We knew what we were getting ourselves into, Sergeant."

Fin took his lips in a hard, hot kiss that was way too short. "I'd like you to avoid getting shot again. But guards, vamps, and shifters are most likely waiting for us as soon as those doors open."

Vaughn almost broke eye contact when he saw the desperation in Fin's eyes. He felt a tug at his lab coat and lowered his gaze to Aaron's pale face.

"Again, you don't have to protect me. I can fight my own way out. I don't want either of you hurt because of me."

Fin groaned. "Damn. He's too cute for his own good." He ruffled Aaron's pale hair. "Stay close to us and keep your head down, kid." Fin stepped in front of them, lifting both guns when the elevator doors slid open.

Their worries had been groundless. As empty as the lower lab levels had been, the ground level was hopping. The fire alarm had obviously chased every Dick and Jane from their workplace. People ran around with files under their arms, their lab coats flying behind them as they hurried for the exits. A group of black-clothed guards stood fifteen feet from the elevator and argued with three scientists who wildly waved their arms.

"There *is* no fire," one of the guards said angrily.

A guy in a green coat stabbed the taller man's chest with his finger. "What the fuck? There has to be. The automatic sprinkler system started. My experiment is ruined. Ruined! I worked on that formula for two weeks, you moron!"

"Holy shit," Fin murmured. "Vaughn, hide your gun. With our coats, we won't raise too much attention in this chaos. Follow me, guys."

Vaughn stuffed his gun into his coat pocket and hid his wound under Aaron's file. Aaron remained by his arm. They followed the other personnel as they evacuated the building. Instead of joining the others at the gathering point, Fin led them back to the gas tanker hiding the hole in the fence. They quickly climbed through.

"Fin, you have to carry Aaron. He doesn't have shoes."

Fin didn't look too happy to hear that. With a heavy frown,

he scooped up Aaron and flung the slender guy on his back. "Keep your fangs away from my neck or I'll wring yours."

Aaron let out a faint whimper but tightened his legs and arms around Fin. "I won't. Although you smell tasty in a weird way."

Vaughn gave Aaron's behind a slap. "No snacking on my man."

As soon as Aaron was secure on Fin's back, they took off running for the tree line. Vaughn trailed behind, since his hip hurt like hell. He had trouble breathing, too. Fin and Aaron had reached the forest when a guard dropped down on them from a tree. Vaughn had no idea why the bastard had been hiding in the tree, but he pumped his tired legs harder when he saw Fin struggle against the attacker. Aaron had rolled several feet and was getting back up.

"No! Leave him alone," Aaron yelled.

Fin grabbed for the guard's arm, trying to keep him from going after Aaron, but took a fist to the face and fell flat on his back. Vaughn was close when Aaron let out a snarl too loud and too vicious for someone his size. Vaughn stopped in his tracks when Aaron's eyes turned crimson red. The guy snarled again, revealing deadly sharp fangs.

The guard lay on top of Fin, his fist raised for another punch. He stared at Aaron with a dark expression. "You're smaller than the other fanged freaks."

Vaughn wasn't sure what to do. He was afraid either Aaron or the guard might hurt Fin. No matter how cute the tiny vamp was, if he attacked Finley, Vaughn would take him down.

But Aaron had chosen his target. Hissing, he launched himself at the guard. The impact threw them both off Fin's body. Fin half crab-walked, half slid over the dead wet leaves toward Vaughn.

Vaughn crouched and pulled his mate against his chest.

"I've got you. Are you okay?" He brought his gun around Finley's body and held it trained on Aaron and the guard, just in case.

"I'm not sure," Fin whispered. "Oh, fuck."

Fangs flashed. Fin tucked his face against Vaughn's chest as Aaron plunged his teeth into the guard's neck. From his earlier comment, Vaughn was sure Aaron had never fed from the source before. Xander had described Bailey's attack on London and how the assassin had fed from the human nurse. That tale hadn't sounded nearly as messy as what Aaron was doing, with the poor bastard wriggling underneath him. The guard was easily twice as heavy as Aaron, but he seemed unable to throw off the slurping, growling man.

"He's a baby vamp, you said," Fin hissed. "He won't hurt us. *Nooooooo.* He's cute and nice with his big brown eyes." He winced when the guard let out a blood-curdling scream.

Vaughn felt decidedly queasy.

"At least he picked one of the bad guys as a snack. The guard's a falcon shifter." Fin gagged but caught himself. "We have to pry Aaron away from him before someone hears his screams."

"Yeah. Right. You go and separate him from his liquid lunch."

CHAPTER EIGHT

Fin had been a soldier. He'd waded through a couple of awfully stinky places, and he'd encountered a fair share of heavily bleeding injuries. Hell, as an enforcer for Xander, he'd hurt and killed other shifters.

But sitting beside a blood-covered Aaron while he drove Vaughn's car the fastest way out of Minnesota was another ballgame altogether. He had a hard time trying not to throw up. It wasn't so much the scent that kept him captive, but the memory of screams and the slurping sounds as Aaron drank his fill.

But no matter how traumatized he felt, Fin was sure the whole experience had been worse for Aaron. The slender man was a picture of misery. They'd left Aaron's dirty clothes in the woods and secured him in his blanket before shoving him into the car. But he'd gotten blood on his skin as well.

They'd taken the stolen car to the trailhead, quickly switched to their own vehicle, and sped off. Vaughn lay curled up in the backseat, groaning softly whenever Fin drove over a rough patch. "Babe . . ."

Fin winced. "I'm sorry. We'll make a medical stop as soon as we're far enough away from Minnesota."

"As long as that time comes before I bleed out."

Despite the gravity of the situation, Fin was glad to hear humor in Vaughn's voice. "Stop it, you baby. You said it was only a graze."

"Are you two a couple?" Aaron asked quietly. "How can you be? You're both so tall and strong."

Fin threw him a quick glance and found Aaron regarding him with a shy expression. He hoped he and Vaughn hadn't set themselves up for hero-worship. "Vaughn is my mate," he said proudly.

"What's a mate?" Aaron's delicate blond brows knitted.

Vaughn coughed from the backseat. Fin wondered if it was a cough, a reaction to Fin's claim, or Aaron's question. "Uh, have you heard of shifters?"

"Shifters?" Aaron's eyes widened. "Like the werewolves in the books?"

Vaughn groaned. "Shit. Nobody told you?"

"Told me what?" Aaron's voice quivered. Although his skin was ghostly pale—probably due to shock—his cheeks glowed a healthy pink.

A side effect of feeding so recently? Finley gripped the steering wheel tighter. "We'll explain everything to you. But maybe it's best you tell us how you ended up as one of Taylor's experiments."

"My older brother works for Taylor. The doctor made Cross healthy again." Aaron took a deep, shuddering breath. "I was so happy for him. We grew up poor and never had enough money for health insurance. I've always been sickly, even as a kid. Cross was okay until he turned twenty-five." Aaron sniffled and rubbed a hand over his bloody face. They were in desperate need of a discreet rest stop. "When the doctor's therapy worked on Cross, he convinced Taylor to treat me as well, although I'm not strong enough to be a guard like my brother. That was Taylor's condition for treating Cross. My brother had to sign an employment contract."

If Taylor had made Cross *healthy*, then he'd been turned and killed people for a living now. Aaron thought his brother was a guard? Damn. The little guy was up for a rude awakening. "What did you suffer from?"

"Multiple sclerosis. Cross heard about Taylor's cure and

decided to give it a try. He wasn't as sick as me, and I think he did it mostly for me, to see if it worked before he put me through the process. He's a great big brother. Cross worked for Taylor without payment for one year to pay for my cure."

"You're fully healed?" Fin asked.

"Yeah. At least the doctor said so." Aaron rubbed his hands up and down his skinny arms. "But . . . something must've gone wrong. I . . . I attacked a man. And I have . . . weird urges ever since I went through the treatment."

Fin was torn. On the one hand, he wanted to strangle Cross for allowing Taylor to turn his baby brother into another species, one that craved blood. On the other hand, he guessed he'd have done the same to save the life of a person he loved. He briefly thought of Sheila, but then shoved the thought away.

Vaughn spoke up from the backseat. He sounded tired. "Don't worry, Aaron. We'll take you home with us where you'll meet someone who's like you and your brother. He'll explain everything and help you deal with your new reality."

"Let me guess—I slid right down the rabbit hole?" Aaron's laugh was shaky. "Shifters, huh? What are you guys?"

Fin sighed. "I'm a cougar, and Vaughn's a coyote. I live in a pride in Nebraska. That's a group of cat shifters."

"Cool. Fin? I really want to wash off the blood. It freaks me out," Aaron whispered.

"I know, little one. How old are you?"

"Seventeen. You . . . you called me a baby vamp back at the lab." Panic laced Aaron's voice. "Did Doctor Taylor make me a vampire? I guess they must be real, too, since you're shifters. I'd much rather Taylor had turned me into a shifter instead of a vampire." He sniffled. "Maybe a cute bunny or something. I don't want to hurt people. Do you think I killed him?"

Fin's heart cracked. "I'm so sorry. We shouldn't have called you that. Bailey—he went through the same treatment as you—doesn't care for that term. But we don't know how to describe what . . ." He bit his tongue.

"To describe what I am," Aaron said quietly. "It's okay. I'd love to talk with this Bailey. Does that mean natural vampires don't exist? Only guys like me?"

"All of them were turned in Taylor's labs. Bailey can give you the details." Fin spotted a sign for a truck stop and left the road. The parking lot wasn't huge and was mostly deserted. He parked the car in a darker corner of the lot and looked around. "Perfect. A side entrance leads to the rest rooms and showers for the truckers. We don't need to drag our bloody asses through the shop area." He turned in his seat and took in Vaughn's curled up form. "Babe?"

"I'm alive. We need the green bag with the medical kit and spare clothes from the trunk." Vaughn sat up with a groan. "You have to clean the wound."

Finley pushed the door to the restroom open and held it with one shoulder while he supported Vaughn's weight with the other. "Hurry, Aaron."

Instead, Aaron wedged his shoulder under Vaughn's armpit and helped Fin wrestle him inside.

Vaughn grunted, his face a mask of annoyance. "It's just a graze. At my hip. I didn't lose my leg, guys."

"Hush." Fin helped his mate over to a wooden bench and lowered him carefully. He straightened and looked around. The room was tiled from floor to ceiling in a cold, slaughter-house-style white. Fin shivered at the thought. At least it was surprisingly clean. He flipped the lock so they wouldn't be disturbed.

A squeal from Aaron pulled his focus from his surroundings. The guy flung his blanket back and hurried to the far wall. Four shower heads were attached to the wall, with four buttons underneath to control the water. Aaron pushed the metal button with both hands and let out a squeak as water pelted him.

"Cold cold cold!" Aaron danced from one foot to the other but remained under the spray.

Vaughn chuckled. "Soap's in my bag."

Fin bent down and searched until his hand closed around the bottle. He pulled it out and tossed it to Aaron, who caught it with a grin. "Come on, sweets. We need to peel you out of your clothes and clean the wound." He squeezed Vaughn's shoulder.

Vaughn looked up at him. Although a smile curled his lips, his eyes were filled with pain. "You want me to strip while the kid watches?" He dipped his head at a wiggling, singing Aaron. "That's so wrong."

The guy was completely oblivious to them as he covered himself in a layer of soap bubbles. A crown of suds topped his head. Shaking his hips, he sang a catchy tune Fin had recently heard on the radio.

Fin smiled. "I don't imagine he'd mind the eye candy, stud. He's a teen on the edge of adulthood who probably knows how to browse for Internet porn." He lowered his voice. "Don't you think he watches porn? At seventeen I'd have done it, but the pack didn't have Internet back then."

"None of our business. Aren't you jealous?" Vaughn shrugged out of his checkered shirt. "Don't know if I should be offended or not."

"Aww." Fin leaned down and dropped a kiss on Vaughn's wild curls. He loved the absolute disarray as well as the silver strands. He lowered his voice. "He's a boy. Let him look. You're mine."

"Am I?" Vaughn quirked an eyebrow and fiddled with the fastening of his vest.

Fin urged his fingers away and opened the vest with a quick yank. "Yeah." He peeled Vaughn out of the vest, then pulled the white undershirt up and over his head. "Damn, I love your hairy chest."

Vaughn rolled his eyes and pushed himself up from the bench seat. "My hip's throbbing like hell. I want to rip that bastard's head off."

Fin took Vaughn's hands and placed them on his shoulders for balance. "Hold on." He hooked his index finger under the waistband of Vaughn's pants and pulled him closer.

"No skivvies," Vaughn warned.

Smirking, Fin popped the button. He slid his hand slowly inside Vaughn's pants and cupped his soft package, shielding it from the zipper as he lowered it carefully. "Don't want to damage the goods," he murmured.

Vaughn's lids fluttered, and he swayed lightly, tightening his hold on Fin's shoulders. "Tease," he hissed through clenched teeth. Vaughn pushed into the hold, his cock plumping in Fin's warm hand. "We can't do this while Aaron's around."

Fin placed his free hand on Vaughn's hip and carefully peeled down one side of his pants. "Thought I'd try to distract you from the coming pain."

"What — Ow!"

"Your pants are stuck to you with dried blood."

Vaughn groaned. "Get it over with."

Fin walked backward and urged Vaughn to follow him until they stood under a shower head. He positioned himself so his body shielded Vaughn's and pressed the button, hissing when the chilly spray hit his back. "Fuck. Give it a second to warm up, then we'll switch." His soaked clothes made the cold worse.

"You could've had my shower." Aaron stood shivering, his arms wrapped around his wet, skinny body.

Vaughn dipped his head. "I have microfiber towels in my backpack."

"Oh, thank God." Aaron hurried over and knelt beside the bag.

Fin snorted and spun Vaughn in a half-circle. "He's not shy. Is the water warm enough?" He slid one hand down Vaughn's chest. The curly hair plastered against Vaughn's skin had turned a darker shade of red. Aaron's presence alone kept him from leaning in and closing his lips around one of Vaughn's tiny pink nipples. He didn't mind being naked in front of others, but Vaughn was right. Aaron *was* still under-age.

"It's fine." Vaughn closed his eyes and tipped his head back, letting the spray hit his hair. He groaned quietly. "Actually, it's pretty amazing. I feel grimy."

Fin hummed and concentrated on Vaughn's pants. The warm water had helped to soften the scab over his wound, so Fin had no problem peeling the fabric down Vaughn's hips. He found a seeping wound of four inches that started at Vaughn's hip bone and ran in a straight line toward his back. "Okay. Let's clean you up and get you moved out of the water as soon as possible. The warm water cleans the wound, but it also causes more bleeding." He looked over his shoulder. "Aaron? Please hand me the soap."

Covered in the thin towel, Aaron hurried over and handed him the bottle. He crouched on the floor and helped Vaughn shake his feet out of the wet pants. "What do you want me to do with this?" He stood and held up the dripping garment.

"Toss it," Vaughn said. "I have sweatpants in the bag that won't put as much pressure on my injury as camos. But can you get some for Fin too, please? And two shirts."

Aaron smiled. "Sure thing!"

Finley made quick work of soaping and rinsing Vaughn's body from head to toe. "All right. Come on." He helped Vaughn back to the bench and looked up into his mate's eyes when Vaughn touched his cheek.

"Hand me the first aid kit. You need to lose the wet clothes and warm up. I don't want you to get sick." Vaughn brushed his thumb over Fin's cheekbone. "I'm serious. I've taken care of a wound before. Trained nurse, remember?"

Turning his head, Fin kissed Vaughn's palm. "Aaron? I trust you to help Vaughn while I clean up real quick."

Aaron nodded and immediately stopped drying his long hair. He tied the towel around his waist and took the first aid kit he'd obviously retrieved earlier to Vaughn. "What do you need?"

While Aaron followed Vaughn's quiet instructions, Finley yanked off his wet clothes, cursing because the material stuck to his skin. Once he was naked, he jumped under the shower and washed up. He shuddered at the sight of the pink water gurgling down the drain. He thanked the Fates he and Vaughn were still alive, but the battle they'd fought today was nothing compared to the war they were still facing.

Fin focused on Vaughn, who patiently showed Aaron how to affix a gauze pad over his wound. One or both of them might get hurt in the future. Hell, some of his friends might lose their lives if they fought against Thoreau and his assassins. As soon as they were back home, he'd grab his mate and snuggle with him—preferably in his own bed. Because only fate knew how much time they'd have with each other.

CHAPTER NINE

Vaughn climbed out of the car and was immediately hit by a small body. He groaned when the impact of Romeo's hug pushed him back against the side of the car, putting pressure on his hip. "Easy, kitten."

Romeo looked up at him with wide eyes. "What? Are you injured? Oh my God, Jules, Vaughn's hurt!"

Romeo's mate appeared behind him and carefully peeled Romeo off Vaughn's chest. "Give him some space to breathe. I'm sure he'll be fine, since he's standing on his own two feet." Jules rubbed up and down Romeo's back.

Vaughn smiled at the two half-pints. "Jules is right. Where's Bailey?" He turned and looked at Fin over the car's roof. His mate was busy hugging Xander while Asa tried to wriggle in between. His fellow enforcers Jaxon and Malcolm stood behind Xander.

"Bailey?" Romeo asked and pulled Vaughn's concentration away from his mate. The ocelot shifter squinted through his thick-rimmed glasses. "Do you need him because your injury is worse than you want to admit?"

"Nope." Although he wouldn't say no to a shot of antibiotics. Gunshot wounds always held the risk of infection, even for a fast-healing shifter. Fin would force him to visit Bailey anyway. "I have someone in the car who . . . well . . ."

"Who?" Jules craned his neck and tried to see through the blackened windows of Vaughn's SUV. "Where did you find them?" His eyes widened. "Did you free someone from the lab? Romeo suggested it, but I never thought you'd actually go against Xander's orders."

Romeo snorted and crossed his arms over his chest. "Right. As though my friend follows anyone's rules but his own. Vaughn's a badass. A fighter. A—"

"He's in trouble, is what he is."

Vaughn turned quickly and came face to face with a scowling Xander.

The alpha's eyebrows were knitted as he gave Vaughn a once-over, his focus lingering briefly on the bulge at his hip. Sighing, he placed one arm around Vaughn and pulled him into an awkward half-hug. Xander patted his back. "Glad you're back in one piece."

"Me, too." Vaughn coughed, surprised at the alpha's touchy-feely greeting. "I brought you a gift." He urged Xander back a couple of steps and opened the door to the backseat. "Come on, Aaron. You're safe." He peeked inside the car and gave him an encouraging smile.

Aaron returned the smile, although it looked forced. He slowly climbed out of the car, tugging at the huge shirt that looked like a dress on him. Thick, woolen socks covered his feet, and his legs stuck out of a pair of Finley's long thermo underpants. Aaron had been cold during the whole ride home although Fin had turned the heat to maximum.

Xander stared at Aaron. He sniffed none too subtly and shot Vaughn a questioning look. "He isn't a shifter." Asa appeared beside his mate and looked at Aaron curiously.

"Nope. He's . . . like Bailey."

Xander snapped his gaze back to Aaron, eyes wide with wonder. "But . . . he's so cute. Why would Taylor . . ." Xander yelped when Asa elbowed him between the ribs.

"I'm the only guy you're allowed to call cute." Asa pursed his lips as he took in Aaron's shivering form.

Vaughn moved one arm around his new friend and tugged him against his side. Aaron shuddered in his arms. "Be nice,

Asa. He's completely innocent. He has no idea what happened to him." He ran his hand over Aaron's silky hair. "I think it's best to introduce him to Bailey. Aaron has questions I can't answer. Bailey might be able to help him. And . . . Aaron might need a snack sooner or later."

Xander nodded and offered Aaron his hand. "Welcome to Wildcat Hills, Aaron. I'm Xander Powell, the alpha of this pride."

When Aaron looked up at him, Vaughn elaborated. "That means he's the head honcho." His wink made Aaron chuckle.

Xander coughed. "That's true. But it also means I'm responsible for your safety and well-being. We'll find you someplace to stay and fetch clothes for you. If you need anything, my door is always open."

Aaron stared at Xander with an open mouth. He snapped it shut, and a blush stole up his neck to the tips of his ears. "Thank you," he said meekly. He grabbed a strand of his hair and nervously curled the tip around his finger. "But . . . why are you so nice?"

Xander gifted Aaron with a warm smile. "Because you're my guest."

Vaughn had to admit he'd never met an alpha like Xander. While he admired Donavan for his strength and determination, he knew the coyote alpha was strict with his pack members. Xander possessed a rare gift of empathy for being such a powerful shifter. Calming a skittish Aaron seemed as easy to him as barking orders to his enforcers.

Aaron finally placed his slender hand in Xander's and smiled. "Thank you. This is very new to me. I'm a little overwhelmed."

"I understand." Xander patted Aaron's hand. "How old are you?"

"Seventeen."

Xander raised his gaze to Vaughn. "I think it's best he stays

96

with you and your mate. At least until he's met the rest of the pride and feels more comfortable around us."

"With . . . me and my mate?" Vaughn choked.

Xander smirked. "I wasn't born yesterday. Why do you think I allowed Alan to meddle? I hope the mission put some things into perspective for you."

Vaughn fisted his hands. "You knew?"

Asa blew a raspberry. "The big lug knows everything. Even before I know! It's annoying." He rolled his eyes and flicked his multi-colored hair out of his face. "But you gotta love him because he's cute." Asa plastered himself against Xander's chest and smacked a loud kiss on his neck.

Aaron giggled behind his hand. "I like you. Your hair is the bomb."

Asa grinned. "Hey, we're the same size, although your legs are much shorter. Want to come with me and check out my closet?" He hooked his arm through Aaron's. "If we don't find anything, we can ask Kei. My stepson is the biggest clothes hoarder you'll ever meet."

Vaughn cleared his throat. "Before you whisk him away, I want to introduce him to Bailey."

Aaron clung to Asa's arm. "Can I meet him after another shower? And I'd like to dress in something my size."

While Vaughn was hesitant to let Aaron out of his sight, Xander squeezed his shoulder. "Let him go with Asa, Vaughn. It'll be good for Aaron to make friends right away. My mate will make sure the whole procedure doesn't take more than an hour, right?" He leveled a hard stare at Asa.

The butterfly shifter pouted. "Aww. Fine."

Vaughn coughed. "Alpha, you might want to send an enforcer with them. Aaron . . . had an accident with one of the guards." When Aaron lowered his gaze and blushed, Vaughn raised his hands. "Not that I don't trust you, Aaron. But you're newly turned. I'm sure you don't want to hurt anyone."

Aaron nibbled his bottom lip and shot Asa a shy look. "That's true."

Xander nodded. "Djimon, go with them. Escort Aaron to Finley's once my mate is done with him."

Asa dragged Aaron away, chattering animatedly about Aaron having to meet Kei and his triplets. Djimon followed them, an amused smile on his face.

Vaughn sighed.

Finley came up beside him and gave him a nudge. "Let's get you home and on the sofa. You need to rest. I texted Bailey to come over and look at your wound."

"How bad is it?" Xander asked, concern ringing in his voice.

Vaughn shrugged. "A graze." He cleared his throat. "My stuff is at Romeo's."

Finley stiffened beside him. The easy smile dropped off his face and was replaced by a blank mask. "You prefer to stay with them?"

"I . . . no. That's not what I meant." Vaughn ran a hand through his hair. God, he was tired.

Fin took a step back. "What *did* you mean?"

To Vaughn, those inches separating them felt like a canyon. "Well . . ." If he stayed with Fin it would feel as though he'd moved in. Permanently. While they'd been on the mission, it had been normal to share a room and the tent. Living with Fin meant a shared bed. And sex. Sex in Finley's bed. Like a real couple. His heart sped up, and sweat popped up on his forehead. Vaughn met Fin's gaze, and the hurt in those brown eyes felt like a fist closing around his heart.

Groaning, Vaughn grabbed Fin by his jacket and pulled him against his chest. He dipped his head and took Fin's lips in a deep, toe-curling kiss. Vaughn was aware everyone around them—his friends, Fin's alpha, and his fellow enforcers—were witness to his downfall. But he didn't care. Although he was scared shitless to open his heart again, to trust another man, he was more afraid of hurting Finley with his attitude.

Xander let out a cough.

When Vaughn tried to break the kiss, Fin wrapped his arms around his neck and held on tight. Breathing harshly, he licked and nibbled at Vaughn's lips as though he was a starving man. He slid his fingers into Vaughn's hair and grabbed his curls, letting out a pleased purr.

"Holy shit," Vaughn muttered under his mate's onslaught. If he weren't injured, he'd have lifted Fin and rutted him against the SUV, their audience be damned.

"Guys?" Xander sounded amused. "Go and get a room. But I expect you both back in an hour to give me a full report. Don't think I forgot that you ignored my order to check in with me daily."

Fin finally wrenched his lips from Vaughn's, gasping for breath. His cheeks were flushed and his pupils big black pools of desire. "Mm hm." He licked his lips slowly, as though to savor Vaughn's taste. The gesture made Vaughn incredibly hard.

Vaughn cleared his throat. He pulled his cell out of his pocket and placed it in Xander's hand. "I suggest you have Romeo check my cell. Hell, let him check the electronic devices of everyone who was aware of our whereabouts. There was a vamp waiting for us at the motel in Minneapolis."

Xander growled. "Dammit. Romeo! My office. Now. And bring your mate." He looked at Finley. "I'll have to reduce your alone time to half an hour maximum. Sorry." He turned and stalked off, snapping his fingers at Malcolm and Jaxon, who followed quickly.

Finley placed a hand in the middle of his chest. "I'll grab our bags. Can you walk? My house is that one, just across the square." He pointed at a cute green single-story house with white shutters and empty flower boxes in the windows.

"It's neat the enforcers have houses on the square, close to the leader." He waited until Fin had gotten their bags, then started limping toward Finley's home. "At Don's pack, the betas and enforcers live in the alpha's house. That's caused some tension over the years."

Fin curled one arm around his waist. "Understandable. Enforcer Jaxon and his mate Viggo stay at the outskirts of the village. But that's okay because Jaxon has impeccable hearing as a deer shifter. He's one of our outposts."

Vaughn grunted as he hobbled up the stairs to Finley's porch. "Do you think Aaron will be okay?" *I hope he keeps his fangs to himself.*

"No idea. But being friends with Asa will help him immensely. Asa is a sweetheart and loved by everyone in the pride. If people see them together, they'll realize Aaron's no threat." Fin opened the door to his home and helped Vaughn inside.

Although Vaughn had known where his mate lived, he'd never been inside Fin's house. The whole place smelled like Finley. It was so intense, Vaughn's dick took notice and twitched in his sweatpants. He shuffled his feet across the gleaming dark hardwood floor. The entrance area was painted a light brown. Vaughn spotted a padded bench, a wardrobe, and a row of jackets on mismatched hooks. A rack held various boots. No dress shoes in sight. Through a door on the right, Vaughn saw a kitchen with shockingly red cabinets.

Once they'd toed off their shoes, Fin gently tugged him through a door on the left that led to the living room. Colorful plush rugs covered the floor. Fin had painted one wall a soft gray while two were white. Vaughn immediately loved the fourth wall that was natural stone and included a fireplace.

Vaughn sank into a tan sofa overflowing with pillows, his

heavy body close to vanishing within the comfy material. "Wow. This is . . . cozy." He carefully wriggled around.

Fin coughed. Was that a blush on his face? "Well, I'm a cat. We love lying around in soft, warm places."

"Oh?" Vaughn raised one eyebrow. "Do you have a favorite cougar-sized windowsill for your afternoon naps?"

Fin flipped him the bird.

"A secret catnip stash?"

"Oh, don't make fun of catnip. It's weed for cat shifters. Honestly. When Kei drank some catnip tea, he freaked out and totally ravaged his mate. That's how Djimon became pregnant." Fin fluffed one of the pillows. "Lie down. I'm sure Bailey will be here in a moment."

Vaughn stretched out on the sofa and groaned appreciatively. "Damn, that's good." When Fin brushed his fingers through his hair, Vaughn closed his eyes. *Hmm.* He'd forgotten how nice it was to be pampered. Not that Walter had pampered him often. To be fair, Vaughn hadn't allowed it.

Reaching up, Vaughn took Finley's hand and opened his eyes. He linked his fingers with Fin's and urged him to take a seat beside him. Fin's expression was tender as he rested his free hand in the middle of Vaughn's chest. He did that a lot.

"Hey, stalker" Vaughn whispered.

"Hey." Fin rubbed his chest, leaned down, and nudged his nose against Vaughn's. He kissed the tip of his nose and his forehead. "Thank you."

"What for?"

Fin's eyes shone brightly. "Staying with me. Allowing me to take care of you."

"I hate being weak."

"Even with me?"

"Especially with you," Vaughn muttered. "Wouldn't you feel the same?"

Fin was quiet for a moment. He squeezed Vaughn's

fingers. "No. I've never felt stronger than when I show you my biggest weakness."

"What *is* your biggest weakness?"

Fin met his gaze. "I thought that was more than obvious."

Vaughn swore his heart skipped a beat. And every beat that followed belonged to Finley Palmer. "Fin . . ." He cupped his mate's cheek, slid his hand behind Fin's head, and kissed him softly. He smiled against Fin's lips when a rumbling purr filled the space between them. Vaughn wanted to say more, but a knock at the door ruined the moment.

Fin sighed. "Damn. It's Bailey. Hold that thought." He got up and left the living room.

Vaughn groaned. He quickly snatched a pillow and pressed it over his groin. "Fucking Bailey."

"Thanks for the offer, but I'm not too keen on another fight with Finley. We already had the pleasure." Bailey was dressed in a white coat and carried a real doctor bag, looking like a country practitioner straight out of a TV series.

Vaughn growled. "Yeah. I heard. Touch my man again, and you'll be in serious trouble."

"Oh, a grumpy patient." Bailey's stupid smile made him way too handsome in Vaughn's opinion. He sported the muscular frame of a linebacker under his coat. His pale silver eyes were exotic as hell, and the silver hair and stubble gave him a distinguished look many men and women appreciated.

"I'll show you grumpy." Vaughn crossed his arms over his chest.

"Let me take a look at your hip." Bailey opened his bag and snapped on a pair of gloves. Vaughn winced at the snap of the rubber.

Fin stood by his head and touched his shoulder. "Don't drag this out unnecessarily. Xander's waiting for us."

Vaughn swallowed. His prick was still hard from the kiss he and Fin had shared. If he took off his pants . . ."It's a nick."

He entered into a staring match with Bailey, determined to win. But when the doc's eyes turned red, Vaughn held up his hands in surrender. "Fine. I hope the scent of blood doesn't bother you. If you think you can snack on me, you've got another thing coming."

"Especially if you think of snacking on him down under," Fin said dryly.

Bailey laughed. "No, thanks. I'll have a look, maybe disinfect the wound again, to make sure you don't get an infection. Now lose the pants."

Vaughn lifted the pillow off his middle. He rolled to his uninjured side and peeled the pants down his hip without revealing too much. But the wound was near his hip bone, so of course Bailey had a peek at the end of his red happy trail. And his unruly cock still pushed against the fabric of the pants.

Bailey smirked. "Happy to see me? Do you have a doctor kink?"

"Shut up."

"I'm sure Finley can buy a sexy nurse uniform online." Bailey winked and concentrated on the wound. He prodded and poked until Vaughn snarled. "Looks okay. The graze, not your dick." Bailey snickered. "Although it's impressive. I'll still give you a shot." He searched through his bag and came up with a syringe and a glass bottle.

Vaughn swallowed as he watched Bailey stick the needle through the bottle cap. The doc held the bottle upside down and filled the syringe. He flicked the syringe with his finger and pressed out the air bubble at the top.

"I hate injections," Vaughn muttered. He realized it was a necessary evil, but still . . .

Bailey pursed his lips. "Don't be such a pussy. It's a little poke. Roll on your belly."

Fin snorted. "I'll remember that line for later use."

"Whose side are you on?" Vaughn glared first at his mate,

then at Bailey. "And where do you think you're going to stick that needle?"

"I need a fleshy, soft spot. Your ass cheek's the best choice."

Vaughn growled, rising up on his elbows. "My ass is not soft!"

"I'm sure he didn't mean it like that," Fin said hurriedly.

"Yes, I did. Belly. Now."

Vaughn did as the doc said. "I'll take my revenge some-day."

Bailey rubbed a wet cotton ball over his left ass cheek for much longer than Vaughn thought was required. Finally, he uncapped the syringe with his teeth. "Oh, I'm so afraid."

"Hey Doc? How's Malcolm?" Vaughn asked. "Do you two still bicker like an old married couple, or has he finally put you out of your misery and fucked — ow!" Vaughn shot Bailey a shocked look over his shoulder.

Fin hissed. "Was that necessary?"

Bailey pulled the needle out of Vaughn's flesh and smirked. "You had it coming." He leaned toward his bag and retrieved a red sucker that he handed Vaughn. "Cherry-flavored fits the occasion. You were a good boy."

"Fucker." Vaughn snatched the treat and ripped off the plastic. He stuck the sucker in his mouth and hummed. "'s good."

Bailey covered the wound with a big square band-aid. "All done. The band-aid will be fine under the shower, but please don't take a long soak in the tub until next week. Keep the band-aid in place for a couple of days. After that keep the wound uncovered. It'll be better for the healing process. If the skin around the site becomes hot or itchy, please call me immediately." Bailey took off his gloves and snapped his bag shut.

"Wait." Vaughn looked at Finley. "Fin was injured as well. Can you take a look at his arm?"

Fin's eyes widened. "No, it's fine. You traitor! You only want to see me getting poked in the ass too."

Vaughn choked. "Don't . . . that's . . . God, no!"

"That came out wrong." Fin's face turned an interesting shade of deep red while Bailey burst out laughing.

CHAPTER TEN

"I received news concerning the whereabouts of our dear friend Hector," Jules said as he threw a folder on the conference table. He took a seat beside his mate and tugged at his silver blue waistcoat.

Xander didn't stop filling an endless row of coffee cups at the head of the conference table. "Is the source reliable?"

Enforcer Jaxon took the filled cups and placed them in front of everyone sitting at the table. Finley sat to Vaughn's right. On his left was Malcolm, who sat beside Bailey. Beta Alan sat to Xander's right. Armand Dubois, future ex-president of the European Shifter Council, was still a guest at Donavan's pack and couldn't attend the meeting. Vaughn was glad, because he didn't know if he trusted the guy yet.

Jules nodded, drumming his fingers on the table. "As a diplomat, I have friends in most states. One of my contacts spotted him in St. Louis. I trust the source. Hector and two of his herd mates are hiding in a shithole of an abandoned house."

Vaughn pursed his lips and focused on Xander. "Do you want us to go and arrest him, Alpha?" Hector, a deer shifter, had captured Asa, who managed to escape with Jaxon's help. Later he'd kidnapped Xander, drugged him, and sold him to a circus in his shifted form when Xander had gotten wind of Hector's illegal activities. Hector had followed the men to Wildcat Hills to recapture them and ship them to Taylor for his weird experiments. The shithead had fled during a raid.

Xander sat down heavily and poured milk into his coffee.

He stirred slowly. "Did your contact tell you anything else? For example, what Hector's doing?"

"Like caging people?" Jules opened the file. "Nope. According to my contact, the group sells drugs to scrape by." Jules slid some photos across the table.

Vaughn snatched one. The man in the photo looked in dire need of a shower and a haircut. His clothes were grimy. "Hector, baby, it looks as though daddy doesn't love you anymore."

Fin leaned against his arm and gazed at the picture. "True. Guess Thoreau cut him off."

"Maybe," Xander said. "Jules, can your contact keep an eye on Hector?"

Jules nodded.

Jaxon spoke up. "You don't want to question him?"

Xander sighed and ran a hand through his hair. "I think he can't tell us anything we don't know. Hector needs to be punished for his crimes. But we can't afford to send someone to fetch him. I'll ask Donavan for help. Vaughn and Fin, it's time for your report."

Fin sipped his coffee, then took a cookie from the plate in the middle of the table. "The operation is much bigger than a couple of months ago when Bailey was at the lab. They upped the security. More cameras, more lights, more guards." He slid the flash drive toward Romeo, who grabbed it and connected it to his laptop. The geek started punching his keyboard right away.

"What's that?" Xander asked.

"We took photos of everything and everyone." Fin cleared his throat. "And Romeo gave us the flash drive to . . ." He shot Vaughn a helpless look.

Xander pinched the bridge of his nose. "Romeo, we'll discuss this later."

"This is on me," Vaughn said. "We have no idea what's on

the flash drive, but it should give us some insight into the whole operation. Oh, we had the pleasure of meeting Zane Taylor. He's a haughty little shit."

Xander's eyes widened while several people around the table gasped.

"What did you do to him?" Jaxon asked. The tall Native American arched one black eyebrow.

"Punched him in the face," Vaughn deadpanned. "And I'm not sorry. Look, Xander. Taylor will inform his fuck-buddy Thoreau about our visit and that we took Aaron. It might scare them enough to relocate the operation."

Xander scratched his stubbly chin, a thoughtful look on his face. "Yeah. And if they do, we'll surprise them. Romeo?"

"On it. I'll hack every available traffic camera closest to the compound. I have a friend who might be able to help me with air surveillance." Romeo tapped away at his laptop, shaking his head. "I ought to kick my butt. Should have thought of this sooner. I also updated the security on our devices. The Department of Security has an awesome hacker who was able to track Vaughn's secure cell. That explains the visiting assassin." Romeo looked at Vaughn through his black-rimmed glasses.

"It was a woman," Finley said quietly.

Xander cursed. "Female assassins. Who'd have thought?"

Alan raised his hand. "Obviously, Taylor doesn't discriminate. I want to drive to Donavan's and give him an update on the assassins as soon as possible. Armand and Raine need to know as well. Romeo, I want you to come with me and take a look at the pack's cells and computers. Until that's done, nobody will make a call to the coyote pack or send them any messages."

Romeo nodded, not once taking his eyes off his laptop as he typed with lightning speed.

Xander leaned back in his chair and nodded. "We need to

discuss Aaron."

"Yeah," Fin said. "And who's gonna tell Aaron his brother is our enemy?"

Vaughn rubbed Fin's back. They both liked the little guy and didn't want to see him hurt. "Tough task. Aaron's older brother, Cross, went through Taylor's *cure* to help Aaron. Both brothers suffered from Multiple Sclerosis. Cross is Aaron's hero. Hearing his brother is an assassin will break his heart."

Xander gazed at Bailey. "What do we know about Aaron's brother?"

Bailey ran a hand over his short gray hair. "Cross Shepherd belongs to Thorne Wilder's team. He's not as crazy as Thorne, but he's still a ruthless killer. Even if he only does it for his brother." He turned to Vaughn. "I wonder why Taylor agreed to turn Aaron, if he's as tiny as you said."

"Because he looks innocent enough to get close to a target?" Xander crossed his arms over his chest. "If a killer's after you, you look out for someone who appears dangerous. Strong. A guy like Bailey or Malcolm, not a cutie like Aaron."

Bailey frowned. "You think Aaron's the first in a new *series* of assassins?"

"Here's his file." Vaughn pushed it over the table toward Bailey. The doc flipped it open and leafed through it. "Whatever Taylor planned to do with him, he didn't have enough time. Aaron was terrified when we found him. He had no idea what they'd done to him. He wasn't trained the way Xander suggested."

"I agree," Bailey said. "He was turned a couple of weeks ago." He slid his finger over the papers in front of him. "Did he tell you if they fed him?"

Fin shook his head. "He didn't know what he needed until . . ." He shot Vaughn a glance.

"Until he came across an unfortunate guard. Aaron saved

Finley. Dude's much stronger than he looks." Vaughn swallowed and massaged his stomach.

Bailey sighed. "Good. That means he's had a good meal. He must've been starved. An assassin needs blood right after the change. The craving is incredibly painful. I can't imagine what Aaron must've gone through. Still, I need to talk with him."

Vaughn nodded. "As soon as Asa lets him out of his clutches, I guess."

Xander groaned. "The hour's up. Last I saw them, Asa convinced Aaron to take a soak in the tub. Said the guy needed some TLC."

Bailey growled. "He needs to be aware of his new biology more than he needs a spa day. Who's with him besides your half-pint of a mate?"

"Djimon."

Bailey nodded and grabbed a cookie.

Romeo clicked on his laptop, and a second later the big flat screen TV behind Xander lit up. "Let's take a look at the photos Fin and Vaughn took while risking their lives."

Xander cursed quietly. "If only I knew how to lure Thoreau out of the city. We can't fight him in Sioux Falls. Too many humans."

"Don't worry," Bailey said around his bite. "He'll eventually come to you. You shut down Hector's operation. And you sent soldiers to his lab who hurt his mate. The noose is slowly tightening around him. However, we need to know how many soldiers he created. A team consists of five men. Or women. I know of at least three teams, because I trained with those men. But there might be many more. My team was defeated when we attacked you. That leaves two. With Cross and Thorne is Priest Cavendish. He's a former Army Ranger and paramedic. Specializes in knives and everything else that's sharp and deadly." He pushed his cup toward Malcolm who rolled his eyes and got up to re-fill it. "Then there's Kee Bishop. Great with everything that goes boom and a little touched in the head. The last is Lance Darwin. Hand-to-hand combat is his middle name."

"And the other team?" Vaughn filed the information away for later use. He wanted to prepare for an attack. Hell, he'd turn Finley's house into a fortress.

Bailey shrugged. "I'll work with Romeo on the material you pilfered and put something together. With photos and shit. Also makes it easier for Alan to update Don."

Vaughn smirked. "You mean a cute power point thingy with effects?"

Bailey grinned and flipped him off. "Don't forget the sound effects."

"Romeo, how long will it take you to work through the data Fin and Vaughn downloaded?" Xander asked.

"I have to decode everything first. Might take a couple of days. Jules will help me."

Xander nodded. "Get to it. And this time, I expect you to keep me in the loop, you little shit." He laughed.

Romeo blushed and curled his lips inside his mouth.

Vaughn shifted in his seat and hissed when his side twinged. He hurt. And the pain meds Bailey had given him made him loopy. He leaned against Finley's arm and linked his fingers with his mate under the table.

"Alpha?" Fin squeezed his fingers. "I need to take my mate home. He's injured, and we both need a couple hours of sleep."

"Of course." Xander stretched, his tendons popping loudly. "You're dismissed. Bailey, go and find my mate and his charge. Take Aaron to Finley's, but try not to disturb the love birds too much." He winked. "Guess we'll come back to the photos another day."

Finley flipped his alpha off, not something Vaughn's alpha

accepted with a relaxed smile. This pride kept confusing the hell out of Vaughn.

Finley craved his comfy mattress in the worst way the moment he and Vaughn returned to their home. Vaughn dragged his feet beside him and leaned on him heavily. But Vaughn's growling belly forced him to change their course from bedroom to kitchen.

"Okay, let's talk about the red."

Fin frowned as he helped Vaughn take a seat at the kitchen table. "What?"

"Your choice in color is . . . bold." Vaughn looked around. "I mean, really? Mirror finish fronts? I bet these are a bitch to clean."

Sighing, Fin crossed the kitchen to his freezer and retrieved a frozen lasagna in a glass dish. "Yeah. Keeps me awake at night." He laughed. "Something went seriously wrong when I ordered the kitchen. I looked at different colors for the cupboards and picked a soft grayish blue. The sales clerk noted the color code on my order form and I signed. When the kitchen was delivered, I had the shock of my life." He tossed the lasagna in the microwave and turned it to de-frost. "Want a beer?"

"Hopped on pain meds? A water will do."

Fin grabbed two bottles from the fridge and joined his mate at the table. He placed one in front of Vaughn and twisted the cap off the other.

"Why didn't you exchange everything for what you really wanted?"

"Tried. The furniture store refused. The damn clerk fucked up with the color codes and entered the code for fire engine red on my order form instead of the gray I picked. Had no idea when I signed the contract and had no chance to prove I never wanted a red kitchen." Fin shrugged as he looked around the room. "You get used to it."

Vaughn seemed skeptical as he slowly sipped his water. "I think I need more of Bailey's painkillers, because I believe deep down you like the red but are too embarrassed to admit it."

"Now you're exaggerating. The color isn't *that* bad," Fin teased.

Vaughn snorted. "Maybe not the color. But the mirror finish?" He mock-shuddered.

Fin threw his bottle cap at his mate. "I hope you'll manage to cook in my monstrosity of a kitchen. Your cooking is pure magic. I'll be the first overweight cougar shifter in history."

"It's normal to gain weight in a relationship." Vaughn winked. "Just wait until you try my casseroles."

Fin stood when the microwave dinged. "Be careful. Before you know it, you'll come home and find me in a housecoat, with curlers in my hair."

"I'll take some pictures for your friends."

Shaking his head, Fin gave the food another spin in the microwave and retrieved plates and cutlery. He set the table, well aware Vaughn was staring at him. "Something wrong?"

"Quite the opposite. For the first time in forever, everything seems right. It's a bit . . . scary," Vaughn whispered.

Fin cupped Vaughn's cheek and dropped a quick kiss on his lips. "I love you." He smiled when Vaughn flushed and shifted his gaze away. "You don't have to say it back." He slid his free hand over Vaughn's chest, where he felt his heart beat fast and steadily.

"Why?"

Fin straightened and pulled the lasagna out of the microwave. "Because I'd never pressure you—"

"No. I mean . . . why do you love me?"

Frowning, Fin placed the bowl and a big spoon on the table

before he sat down. Vaughn looked helpless and . . . upset?

"I don't get it. Walter loved me because I was young and pretty and I helped him out at the infirmary. He loved that I looked up to him. But you . . . I was horrible. I pushed you away every time you tried to reduce the distance between us. I insulted you." Vaughn raked a hand through his hair. "I can't believe I'm actually revealing my insecurities. What the hell did Bailey shoot me up with?" He tilted his body to the side and rubbed his ass cheek.

Finley bit his lip, since it wouldn't do him any good to laugh. Instead he scooped lasagna onto Vaughn's plate and pushed it toward him. "The food will help with the loopy feeling."

Looking disgruntled, an expression Finley had come to love because it made Vaughn absolutely adorable in his eyes, Vaughn grabbed his fork and stabbed at the food with deadly determination. "So . . . why?" He put a bit in his mouth, his eyebrows climbing up his forehead. "Huh. Tastes exactly like mine."

"Probably because it *is* yours." Fin cleared his throat. "Don't give me that look. Romeo gave me the glass dish when I dropped by the other night. You'd taken it out of the oven and Jules invited me to dinner. You saw me and remembered you had to do laundry. Then you were gone, and I must've looked totally pathetic, hanging shoulders and all, because Romeo gave me the food." He huffed. "He'd kill for your cooking, so you can probably imagine how much your behavior chipped away at my self-esteem for him to let go of the lasagna."

When he met Vaughn's gaze, his mate blinked slowly. The hand holding his fork shook. Suddenly, he let go of the silverware and placed his face in his upturned palms. Groaning, Vaughn placed his elbows on the table. "Turn the knife, why don't you? God, I'm such a shitty mate."

"No!" Fuck, what had he done? Finley rubbed Vaughn's shoulder, trying to soothe him. "I didn't tell you to make you feel bad. I'm sorry."

"*I* should be sorry." Vaughn rasped his palms over his stubbled cheeks. He looked so fucking defeated Finley's heart broke for him.

Finley stood, walked behind his mate's chair, and slid his arms around his chest. He brought his mouth to Vaughn's neck and kissed his pale skin. "I love you because you yelled at me to pull my head out of my ass when I failed to shoot the assassin attacking us."

Vaughn let out a sound between a cough and a grunt. "The fuck? Me calling you an idiot gets you all hot and bothered?"

"We're talking about my feelings, Vaughn, not how fast you turn my dick hard." He rubbed his nose over the soft spot under Vaughn's ear, breathing in his natural musky scent. Finley closed his eyes, humming happily. "It was the first time you showed you were capable of feeling more than annoyance when it comes to me. I saw the fear in your eyes when that bitch shot me. Fear for me. You should've seen your face when you killed her. Before you'd always been so cold and aloof. That look was gone in an instant, replaced by desperation and . . . anguish."

Vaughn reached up and covered Finley's hands on his chest with his. "You're crazy. And I must be crazy as well, because I'm falling for you, kitten."

Chapter Eleven

Finley woke lying half on top of something incredibly warm and hard. Something that moved up and down. He opened his eyes and smiled when he saw the wide expanse of Vaughn's pale, freckled back gleaming in the morning light.

After they'd eaten dinner, they'd barely had enough energy to undress before they tumbled into bed. Finley had been out like a light as soon as his head hit the pillow.

He briefly wondered if Bailey had brought Aaron home. But then Vaughn turned his head and let out a cute snuffling noise, and every thought not concerning his mate fled his mind.

Finley wanted a couple of hours where nothing existed but him and the man he loved. No fighting. No missions. No power-hungry politicians. Just getting to know the mate he'd share his life with from now on.

Finley rested his head in his palm and ran his index finger down the middle of Vaughn's back, loving the silkiness of his skin. Vaughn stretched and flexed, letting out a grunt. Smiling, Finley leaned over him and started kissing from his nape to his shoulder blade while he slid his hand up and down his mate's side.

Feeling adventurous, he licked over Vaughn's shoulder and cute freckles, purring when Vaughn's musky taste exploded on his sensitive tongue. He pressed his front harder against Vaughn's side, loving when his morning wood brushed his mate's skin. As a cat shifter, Fin had always been tactile. He liked to sniff and lick his lovers.

"Want me to grab the lube?" Vaughn's voice was scratchy and deep. "We could take care of your v-card."

Finley laughed and nuzzled the back of Vaughn's neck. "Not everything is about sex." He climbed on top of Vaughn and stretched out until they touched from head to toe. "We haven't had much time for slow exploring."

Vaughn hummed. "You're heavy, and your dick's leaving a puddle on my back. But be my guest and explore away."

"Oh, shut up and let me enjoy what's mine." Finley trailed his fingertips up and down Vaughn's strong arms. The coarse hair on his forearms tickled pleasantly. Eventually, Finley stretched his arms along Vaughn's and linked their fingers.

Vaughn curled his arms and tugged their joined hands under his shoulders. "This is nice."

"Yeah." Finley nibbled on the side of Vaughn's neck. "You smell good in the morning."

"I want to wake up like this every day for the rest of our lives," Vaughn whispered.

"How? Squished into the mattress?" Finley teased. He was quiet for a moment, closing his eyes and listening to Vaughn's strong and steady heartbeat.

A deep sigh from Vaughn moved Fin up and down. "I want to wake up knowing that, although we'll probably fight and argue, you haven't left me."

Fin's breath stuttered. "Vaughn . . . I'm yours. Always have been. Always will be." He nipped Vaughn's nape. "We can make this work, baby. If I ever fuck up, don't hesitate to tell me. Because I sure as hell will tell you if *you* fuck up." He freed one hand and tugged on one of Vaughn's locks, smiling when it bounced right back. "But no matter what happens between us, I'll never leave you."

"I didn't plan to deny you forever, okay?" Vaughn scoffed. "Well, I didn't really have a plan. I denied what I felt and shoved it away so I didn't have to deal with my feelings. I . . ."

He licked his lips. "I'm the worst when it comes to emotional crap." When Vaughn rolled, Finley slid off his back and lay on his side. Vaughn reached for him and pulled him into a kiss. "Do you think . . ."

"What?" He brushed a flaming red strand out of Vaughn's face.

Vaughn caught his lip between his teeth. He circled his fingertips on Fin's hip. "Walter died only a year ago. Do you think . . . were we meant to be together? The three of us? Or did fate match us after Walter died?"

Fin hesitated. He didn't want to offend Vaughn or play down his relationship with Walter, because it was obvious from the intensity of Vaughn's grief that he'd loved his mate more than his own life. "I . . . don't know. To be honest, I never thought much about fate. But . . . I love the idea of fate giving us what we need when we need it most." He looked into Vaughn's eyes, saw the pain and hope battling in his intense gaze. Fin cupped Vaughn's cheek. "Walter will always have a place in your heart. That will never change. I can't tell if fate thought of us as a throuple. I never met Walter, so I don't . . ." He took a deep breath. "I can't miss someone I've never met. I look at you and don't feel as though anything is missing. If *you* feel that way, it's okay. That you love Walter as much as you obviously do makes me love you even more."

Vaughn swallowed, his Adam's apple bobbing. "I was asking because . . . Is it bad I can't imagine him with us? With you?" He closed his eyes for a moment, and when he opened them again, they were wet with unshed tears. "Is it wrong I want you for me?" He tightened his hold around Finley.

Finley slid his hand behind Vaughn's head and pulled his face into the crook of his neck. "No, baby. That's not wrong. It's human."

"I think I love you," Vaughn whispered, then pressed his lips against Finley's shoulder.

It was a moist, sucking kiss that had Finley moaning quietly. "Vaughn . . ." His heart pounded and his mind reeled from the bomb of a revelation Vaughn had dropped.

Vaughn rolled them until he lay on top. "I'd love to see your cougar."

Fin cocked his head. "Now?" Damn, but Vaughn's trains of thought gave him whiplash. Why couldn't they review the l-word incident?

"Well, yes. I want to run with you. Yank the cat's tail." He winked. He dipped his head and nipped Finley's neck. "And when we come back, I want to claim you properly."

"Hmm, sounds good." Maybe it was wise to allow Vaughn an emotional pause. "I've seen some of your pack mates in their shifted forms. Coyotes are so damn cute." He touched the tip of Vaughn's nose.

"Cute?" Vaughn glowered. "I'm not a puppy!"

Leaning up, Fin licked his mate's stubbled chin. "Aww. Don't be a grump." He wriggled out from underneath Vaughn and jumped out of bed. "Let's go. It's been ages since my cougar had some fun." When Vaughn growled low and sat up, Finley took off running. His mate would chase him, since coyotes, as well as wolves, loved a good chase, while cats were known for their stalking.

Finley ran toward the front door, looking over his shoulder when he heard softer footsteps than he'd anticipated on the hardwood floor. He grinned when he saw a coyote running after him. Fin opened the door, then turned to face his mate. "You're beautiful."

Vaughn slithered to a stop in front of Finley. He cocked his head and let his tongue loll.

Finley knelt before him and touched the soft fur between Vaughn's ears. He was more slender and smaller than a wolf. His ears were a smidge bigger, too. And his coat was the same russet and silver color as his human hair. "You're surprisingly soft," he murmured, burying his fingers in Vaughn's fur.

Vaughn yipped and licked his cheek, swishing his tail.

Finley laughed and kissed his mate's snout. "Okay. My turn." Fin concentrated on his cougar and let the change come over him. It always felt like a thorough stretch. Once he stood on four paws, he yawned and arched his back.

Vaughn yipped again and bumped his head against Finley's. Finley delivered a slow lick to Vaughn's head, flattening his fur. Vaughn shook himself from head to tail and growled.

Finley lowered his belly to the floor. Flicking his tail, he watched Vaughn carefully and waited. It was obvious Vaughn had no idea what Fin was doing, because he cocked his head again and let out an adorable whine. He danced on his paws, clearly eager for a run.

Finley wriggled his behind, lifted it in the air, and pounced. Although Vaughn reared back, Fin landed on top of him and they rolled on the floor. When Fin bit Vaughn's ear playfully, his mate yipped. Fin rolled on his back and lifted his front paws into the air, stretching them toward Vaughn.

Vaughn let out a chuffing noise resembling a laugh. He nudged Finley's cheek with his nose and snuffled. Finley purred, loving Vaughn's nuzzling. Before Fin became too comfortable, Vaughn jumped away and ran to the open front door. He turned, barked, and ran off.

Finley rolled to his paws and followed his mate into the cold but sunny day.

When they returned from their run—sweaty, horny, and ready for a romp—they found Bailey and Aaron in their living room. Aaron was curled up in an armchair, dressed in sweatpants and a huge Panthers hoodie.

"How cute." Vaughn chuckled. "Need cookies with your tea? Please, tell me it's tea in those cups and not crimson juice."

"Crimson juice?" Bailey huffed. "Good one. Please, put some clothes on before you poke someone's eye out."

"Intimidated?" Vaughn placed his hands on his hips.

Finley pinched the bridge of his nose. He had no idea why Vaughn loved taunting Bailey so much. And normally he wouldn't mention it, but poor Aaron wasn't used to them. "My mate, why don't you follow Bailey's suggestion before Aaron's eyes fall out of his head? Or do I need to remind you he's seventeen?"

Vaughn groaned. "He's part of a pride now. He has to get used to naked people sooner or later." However, he turned and walked down the hallway, a noticeable sway to his hips.

Finley licked his lips, ready to pounce. But Bailey coughed and broke the spell. Finley grabbed a blanket from the back of the sofa and secured it around his hips before he sat down. "Sorry, but Vaughn's right when he says shifters aren't modest."

"I lived with Malcolm. Believe me, I noticed," Bailey said dryly.

Aaron giggled. "I don't mind. So much eye candy."

"Did you come back yesterday? Where'd you sleep? I'm so sorry Vaughn and I were in our room. We haven't been good hosts." Fin was surprised he hadn't heard Aaron either. Back in the military, he wouldn't have slept through someone entering his house.

"Oh, he stayed at the alpha's house," Bailey said. "Xander wanted to give you and Vaughn time to . . . relax. I just brought Aaron over fifteen minutes ago. We found the door open, so we thought we'd wait for you."

Fin heard the shower start in the back of the house and leaned back. "Ah, that's cool. My home is your home, Aaron. Did you have a good talk so far?"

Aaron nodded, his eyes shining with adoration and pink hearts when he looked at the older doctor. "Bailey is super nice."

Oh, damn. Fin coughed. "That's true. I'm sure you have questions, Aaron."

"Yes! Mostly about my brother. When will I see him again? Can I contact him?"

Bailey leaned forward, hands dangling between his knees. "You have his number?"

"Memorized. I wanted to tell him I'm healthy, but Doctor Taylor wouldn't let me call him." Aaron's bottom lips trembled. "He's not as nice as Cross said he was. I mean . . . the man in the cell next to mine died." He sniffed, rubbing the cuff of his hoodie under his nose.

Finley shot Bailey a helpless look.

Bailey sighed. "Aaron, you need to understand something. Taylor's intention is *not* to cure sick humans. He's no good Samaritan. Taylor works for the president of the shifters in North America."

Aaron's eyes widened. "President? Wow. That means he's important?"

"Very," Finley said. "But the president's not a good guy."

Bailey shook his head. "The president needs soldiers, Aaron. And Taylor delivered them."

"Cross," Aaron breathed. "My brother . . . he's strong. He wanted to join the military when he turned eighteen, but they wouldn't accept him because of his condition." He started trembling. "Cross isn't a guard, right?" Aaron's huge eyes swam with tears.

Bailey shook his head. "I met your brother during our training. We were in the same branch of our profession, little one."

"What profession?" Aaron twirled a strand of hair around his finger until the tip turned white. "Are you soldiers?"

"No, we're assassins."

Aaron gasped. "No." He shook his head rapidly.

"I'm so sorry." Bailey's voice was gentle, soothing. He leaned forward and touched Aaron's knee.

Finley's heart bled for Aaron when he grabbed Bailey's hand and held on tight, as though the doctor was a lifeline. Aaron looked devastated.

Vaughn returned to the living room, smelling freshly showered and dressed in jeans and a long-sleeved shirt. "Hey." He plopped down beside Aaron and pulled him into an embrace.

Finley was so proud of his mate. He hadn't expected his standoffish man to be so touchy-feely, but Aaron had obviously wormed his way through Vaughn's defenses.

Aaron rested against Vaughn and sniffled. "But Cross never hurt a fly."

"It's the *cure*," Bailey spat. "I've always had a temper, but after Taylor's treatment, my aggressive tendencies grew immensely. And the strength I gained after I was turned . . ." He briefly closed his eyes. "It went to my head. I felt invincible. Didn't you notice your brother changing?"

Aaron rubbed his eyes. "I . . . didn't see him much after he started the new job. He was always so busy with work, he arranged for me to move into a care facility. Cross regularly sent money to pay for it. I miss him terribly."

"Bailey?" Fin ran his fingers through his hair. "From what Aaron told us, Cross loves his brother. I guess he stayed in the program because he needed help for Aaron."

"Possible, although I wonder why Cross put Aaron through the change after he experienced it himself." Bailey frowned.

"Love," Vaughn said quietly. He met Finley's gaze. "A man will do everything for his loved ones. I bet he thought having Aaron as a baby vamp is better than losing him."

Aaron clung tighter to Vaughn. "Does that mean Cross is your enemy? You said the president's bad, and my brother works for him."

Bailey shrugged. "I don't know. I left my team during an attack on Xander's pride because I didn't want to kill anymore. Cross might be willing to do the same."

"Maybe he just needs an incentive." Vaughn dipped his head, indicating Aaron.

Aaron looked up at him. "What do you mean? Me?"

"If your brother knows you're safe, there's no reason for him to stay with his team." Vaughn shot Bailey a questioning look. "Right?"

Bailey frowned and crossed his thick arms over his chest. "Yeah. Unless he enjoys his work and it's his loyalty to Taylor that keeps him on the team. We can't risk it."

"Risk what?" Finley looked back and forth between Bailey and Vaughn. "I don't understand."

Bailey sighed. "Your mate wants to allow Aaron to call his brother and tell him where he is. This is *not* the best time for a family reunion. Cross is dangerous, Vaughn. He's Aaron's brother, but he can't be trusted."

"Bailey's right." Finley got up, clutching the blanket around his hips. "Cross might come here and bring his team with him to retrieve his brother." As much as it hurt him to see Aaron's crestfallen expression, as an enforcer he had to take the pride's safety into consideration. "Xander wouldn't allow that."

Aaron quickly shook his head. "I don't want any of you hurt. Kei and the babies . . . Asa . . ." He looked at Bailey. "What about me? I feel okay. No urge to sneak around and kill people." He shuddered. "Well . . . I still feel bad because I hurt the guard. Don't know what came over me."

Bailey shook his head. "You're newly turned, so your emotions will be intensified for a while. Anger. Aggression. Lust. That's normal. You might lose control, similar to your attack on the guard. But you weren't forced through a training program with other highly aggressive men like me or your brother. You have people here, friends, who'll help you balance your feelings."

Aaron blinked. "You want to be my friends? Asa said he wants to be my friend."

"Nah, I want to be your foster dad or something." Vaughn said and ruffled Aaron's hair.

Aaron gasped quietly.

Finley smiled. "You're part of the pride. We're a big family—annoying at times, but always there for you."

Aaron smiled shyly. "I'd love that." He sighed as his smile fell. "I still miss Cross, but I understand you don't know him and you can't trust him based on the fact he's my brother."

Finley pursed his lips. "Taylor's not dumb. It's only a matter of time before he finds the connection between us and Xander. They have us on video, and a warrant is still out for Vaughn in Sioux Falls. He'll figure out where Aaron is, and so will Cross."

"Means he might come anyway." Bailey stood. "I'll bring it up with Xander, see what he thinks. Aaron, I'll come back later to bring you some blood bags. And don't forget to eat solid food as well."

Aaron nodded quickly, shooting Finley a look.

"What are you in the mood for, little one? Vaughn and I haven't had breakfast yet either. Babe, can you whip us something up while I take a shower?"

Vaughn stood as well while Bailey waved and left. "Do you know your way around the kitchen, Aaron? You can be my prep cook."

Aaron scrambled after Vaughn. "Prep cook? For breakfast?"

"You haven't tried my mate's food, pal." Fin laughed and clapped his hand on Aaron's slim shoulder. "He goes all out. I expect a feast upon my return." He pointed his finger at

Vaughn.

Vaughn grabbed Aaron's hand, rolling his eyes. "Aaron, did you know dogs have a master and cats have staff?"

Aaron snickered behind his hand. "Well, sounds to me as though your master has spoken."

Vaughn's eyes widened. "Why, you . . ."

Aaron squeaked and took off running, Vaughn hot on his heels.

Laughing quietly, Finley walked in the opposite direction. Although he'd been looking forward to some naughty fun between the sheets — with Vaughn sweaty and dirty from their run — poor Aaron was in desperate need of some TLC.

They'd rescued the boy, so Finley felt responsible for him. Aaron was too young to stay on his own. Hell, teenagers were ticking time bombs anyway with their raging hormones and mood swings. A teenager who'd discovered shifters, had lived through a dangerous experiment, and would always be dependent on blood from a bag? That was a disaster waiting to happen.

Finley took a quick shower and dressed before he joined his new family in the kitchen. Leaning against the doorjamb, he smiled as he watched Vaughn show Aaron how to cook breakfast. The teen looked skeptical while he dunked a slice of bread into a bowl filled with a sogging mess of whisked eggs and milk.

"Looks gross. Are you sure it's edible?" Aaron crinkled his tiny nose and wriggled his wet fingers slightly.

Vaughn laughed and took over. "Wash your hands and put a frying pan on the stove. Butter's in the fridge. Add a couple tablespoons to the frying pan and turn on the burner."

"What's for breakfast?" Fin pushed off the door and strolled to the coffee machine. The high-end thingy had been a birthday present from Thony after they'd had a lengthy conversation about coffee brands and quality one night over beer.

After the first cup, Finley had wondered how he'd ever lived on cheap grounds. "Coffee?"

"Yes, please." Vaughn lifted the wet bread out of the bowl and placed the slice into the sizzling pan. "Aaron and me are making French toast."

Aaron giggled. "I hope it tastes better than it looks. Can I have coffee too?"

"Uh . . . okay." Fin had started drinking the black juice of the gods when he'd been way younger than Aaron. Maybe he should've asked Bailey about special dietary restrictions.

Vaughn bumped his hip. "Relax, love. Let him have a cup. What's the worst-case scenario? Him bouncing around like a rubber ball?"

Aaron indeed bounced on his toes while he held a cup with both hands and stared longingly at the black liquid Finley poured. "At the care home the nurses never let me have coffee. Cross snuck in a cup occasionally when he came for one of his rare visits." His eyes glistened.

Finley carefully pulled Aaron against his chest without jiggling him and the cup too much. He kissed the kid's hair. "Drink all the coffee you want. Hey, I know nothing about French toast, but I can manage scrambled eggs. Let's enter a breakfast contest. Us against Vaughn."

Aaron looked up at him with a mischievous twinkle in his eyes. "Challenge accepted." He lifted the mug to his lips and took a big gulp. "I'll crack if you scramble." When he lifted his palm, Fin high-fived him, and they got to work beating Vaughn's culinary ass.

It didn't take the three of them long to prepare a huge feast. Aside from the French toast and scrambled eggs, they had bacon, waffles with hot berry sauce, and sausages. Maybe they'd gone a little overboard in their contest, but Aaron turned out to be a typical teenager, small as he was. He was a bottomless pit who shoveled in his breakfast as though he hadn't had solid food for months. From what Finley had read in his file, that was possible.

"You'll need a cup of special juice as dessert," Vaughn said carefully.

Aaron seemed unfazed at the prospect and nodded, his mouth full and cheeks puffed out. "Bailey said the taste is weird at first, so I should think of it as . . . medicine." He stuffed another slice of bacon into his full mouth.

Vaughn shot Fin a quick look. "Good idea. After breakfast I'll show you to . . . your room?"

Fin nodded. "Spare bedroom's on the left at the end of the hall. Opposite a tiny bathroom. We can remodel it, install a new shower. I have fresh sheets in the hall closet."

"Kei and Asa gave me clothes. They're in a backpack in the living room." Aaron smiled shyly. "They're nice guys. I panicked when Kei forced me to hold one of his kids. They're cute but . . . babies." He grimaced.

Fin pointed his fork at Aaron. "Remember that feeling. It will keep your head on straight when you're on a date."

Aaron arched one pale brow. "Now you sound like a dad. Finley, I'm gay, jeez. I find girly bits worse than babies. Oh, hey. Do you have Wi-Fi? Romeo promised he'd get me a tablet packed with games." His cheeks flushed, and he was very focused on the last bite of French toast.

Finley hid his smile with his hand and winked at Vaughn, who seemed to be in the same predicament, because he bit his lip. It didn't matter to him if Aaron needed Wi-Fi for games or something else. He hoped Romeo's tablet came with the best firewall imaginable. Remembering his own youth and how he'd suffered through slow Internet while looking at his first booby pictures, Fin would make sure the device had no child safety lock. The boy was seventeen. Finley wouldn't treat him like a child.

Vaughn sat behind Aaron on the bed and ran a brush through his long, wet hair. He'd been surprised when Aaron had asked for help with a braid, convinced it was a ruse to talk with Vaughn alone.

The guest room was nice but lacking in personality, like most guest rooms. The bed was a queen-size and freshly made. Fin had parted with some of his beloved pillows from the living room in order to make the bed more comfortable. A chest of drawers and a wardrobe topped by a mirror completed the setup. On the wall over the chest hung a TV. Fin had promised they'd take Aaron to the nearest city and shop for some accessories soon.

Parting Aaron's hair in three sections, he hummed quietly.

"I wasn't sure if you'd know how to do this," Aaron said quietly.

A slurping sound told Vaughn Aaron had reached the bottom of the plastic cup holding his liquid snack. Bailey had brought the blood bags earlier and suggested they pour each one into a non-transparent container and add a straw. His idea seemed to work, since Aaron hadn't made a face or complained about the taste. According to Bailey, bagged blood tasted nasty. Maybe it was a question of preference.

"What? Braiding hair?" Vaughn laughed. "I grew up in a coyote pack not far from here. A pack is a huge family, and I used to assist my late partner at our infirmary. Shifter children are a wild lot. They have scrapes all the time, so it's not uncommon for them to show up in the infirmary needing first aid and a little TLC. You learn to braid hair pretty quickly when a six-year-old gives you an eye roll because you told her you can't make a braid." He let the pale blond strands slide through his fingers as he made quick work of Aaron's hair. It was long, very thick, and silky, so he made sure the braid was tight.

Aaron giggled. "Understandable. My mom . . . she loved my hair. After she passed away and Cross took custody of me, I always made a huge ruckus when he mentioned cutting it. Eventually he gave up. The only time I ever let anyone close to my hair is when the ends need trimming."

"We have a hair stylist in the pride. Jaxon's hair is almost as long as yours, so he'll understand. He's a proud Native American and mostly wears his hair loose."

Aaron nodded. "I met Kei's husband. Mate. His curls are freaking awesome." He was quiet for a while and slurped the empty cup. "Vaughn?"

"Yeah?" He wrapped a scrunchie around the end of Aaron's braid and tugged at it.

"Thank you for taking me in. You and Fin have been nothing but nice to me. If I come across as too needy or — "

"Stop right there." Vaughn shuffled on the bed so he sat opposite Aaron. "You're welcome in our home. It's your home too until you decide you want to be somewhere else. As for being too needy . . . nope. You've gone through a lot. I know you miss your brother, he's your only family." He took Aaron's slim fingers between his and squeezed them. "And I imagine living in a care home wasn't a party, either. Whatever you need, simply ask." Although Aaron was seventeen, he hadn't had a chance to be a normal teenager because of his medical condition. He'd told them before Cross went to work for Taylor, he'd had two jobs at the same time to pay for Aaron's medical bills. He hadn't been home much.

Aaron flung himself into Vaughn's arms and held on tight. "Thank you. But if it's too much, you'll tell me?"

"Yeah, but don't expect that to happen. Ever." He ran his hand up and down Aaron's back. When Aaron yawned, Vaughn pulled back and smiled. "Take a nap if you like, or watch TV. Fin has Netflix." He winked. "I'll come and wake you when it's time for dinner." He took the plastic cup and left once Aaron had nodded and grabbed for the remote. When he left the room, Fin was waiting for him in the hallway, his hands stuffed into his pockets.

"How is he?" Fin sounded pensive.

"Tired." He juggled the empty cup. "But sated." Vaughn closed the distance and brushed his lips over Finley's. "You're not . . . jealous because he wanted to talk with me alone, are you?"

Fin placed his forehead against Vaughn's and took a deep breath. "Not in the least. I'm glad he feels comfortable with us. Both of us."

"Then what's with the nervous fidgeting?" Vaughn slipped his index fingers through Fin's belt loops and pulled him against his body.

Fin nibbled his bottom lip. "Well . . . the kid's busy so I thought . . . maybe you'd like to . . . claim me."

Vaughn's breath caught in his chest. "Claim you? As in . . ."

"As in shove your magnificent cock up my ass until we both come harder than we've ever come before while you bite my shoulder." When Fin lifted his gaze, his brown eyes were dark with lust. A lovely blush covered his cheeks, and the scent of Fin's arousal tickled Vaughn's sensitive nose.

"Holy shit." Vaughn let his head fall back and groaned. "Listening to you talk dirty has become my new favorite hobby. Tell me more."

Fin laughed. He slid his strong fingers over Vaughn's pecs and pinched his nipples through his shirt. "Gladly. But first, come with me. No pun intended." Taking Vaughn's hand, Fin dragged him down the hallway, through the kitchen, and toward the back entrance leading to the yard.

CHAPTER TWELVE

"Why did you bring me out here?" Vaughn wrapped one arm around his waist and lifted his free hand to tug up the collar of his jacket. He glanced into the sky, a skeptical look on his bearded face. "Those clouds look heavy with snow. I'd rather be balls deep inside your heat before the white stuff comes down."

Finley stepped up beside his man and looped his arms around him. He pressed a kiss to Vaughn's cheek, lingering a moment to breathe him in and enjoy the warmth of his skin. "Bear with me for one moment. It's a surprise."

"What exactly?" Vaughn turned his head, arching one eyebrow. "The devastating condition of your back yard? Consider me sufficiently surprised. Now, can we go inside so I can pop your cherry?" He pecked Fin's lips.

Fin laughed, squeezing his mate. "Asshole." Although Vaughn was right. His backyard was a yellowish expanse of sickly grass mixed with weeds. Maybe the weeds had overgrown the grass, taken control of it. Fin sighed. "I thought . . . maybe if I toss the trash—and with help from some friends—we can turn the backyard into a garden. I know how much you love to cook with fresh ingredients." He took in the rusting truck wreck with a rotting water barrel beside it. Five feet to the left stood a wheel-less wheelbarrow, filled with brownish, muddy water and dead leaves. His hedges were a nightmare. And he'd never managed to remove the roses that had died three winters ago.

Finley cringed. "I have a brown thumb and never knew

what to do with the place. I'd love a deck where we can grill a steak or something. Maybe a pool? I bet Aaron would love that. We have a community pool behind Xander's house, but it's pretty crowded in the summer and filled with squealing cubs." When he met Vaughn's gaze, his mate gave him an odd look. "What?"

"You . . . you're giving me reign over your yard? I can do with it whatever I want? Toss the trash? Plant vegetables and fruit?"

"Yeah," Fin said carefully. "We need a place to relax, right? My cougar likes to nap in the sun, and I'd love to cuddle up with your coyote." Was Vaughn happy about his gift? Was it lame? "Babe, say something."

A tender smile lit up his eyes and spread over Vaughn's face. "Kitty cat, I love you. That's a great gift. You have to promise me one thing, though — don't touch the plants."

Fin threw back his head and laughed. He shrieked when Vaughn grabbed him around the waist and threw him over his shoulder. "Vaughn! I'm heavy. Your hip . . ."

"I'm fine aside from freezing my nuts off. Considering I plan to use them very soon, you'll have to give them a warm tongue bath." He had the audacity to slap Fin's ass as he carried him back into the house.

"Vaughn Christian! Put me down, right this second." Laughing and feeling light-headed hanging head down like a bat, Fin held onto Vaughn's flexing globes for balance.

"Be quiet! Or do you really want Aaron to sneak around and press his ear against our bedroom door?"

Fin groaned. "You're a bad bad man." He gasped when he went sailing through the air. Fortunately, he had a thick, bouncy mattress. Correction — *they* had a thick, bouncy mattress.

The door slammed shut behind Vaughn. "You can punish me later." Grinning, Vaughn pulled his sweater over his head and threw it aside. He slid his hand — torturously slowly — from his sculptured pec down over his flat stomach to his belt buckle.

"*Fuck.* You're *killing* me." Fin licked his lips. His body felt overly hot. He had a feeling things would get hotter the more clothes they lost. He quickly yanked his shirt and pants off.

"I like your expression when you look at me, stalker." Vaughn's voice dropped to a deep rumble. "No hesitation because I'm a guy. Only lust and need." He quickly unbuckled and unzipped, then shoved his pants down his legs. A sensual stripper he was not, but Finley didn't care.

"The fact you have a cock wasn't a concern when I met and scented you for the first time." Finley took in Vaughn's pale, hairy, muscled body. His curly hair was once again in total disarray, as though they'd already gone several rounds between the sheets. "You're stunning. Inside and out."

Vaughn walked to the edge of the mattress, placed his knee on the bed, and slowly crawled over him. "Are you nervous?"

"I . . . wait." Crunching up, Finley pulled his legs against his chest and fought with his damn socks. "Can't wear socks during sex."

Vaughn snorted. "I won't complain, since I love the position you maneuvered yourself into." Placing his hands left and right of Finley's head, he leaned down and kissed him sloppily. "I want your legs over my shoulders when I fuck you, although on your belly might be more comfortable for you."

"I don't care as long as this" — he curled his hand around Vaughn's shaft — "goes inside me."

Vaughn grunted and peppered his face with kisses. "My fearless sergeant. Lube?"

"Usual place." Fin tipped his head back when Vaughn nibbled along his neck. Closing his eyes, he relished Vaughn's weight on top of him, his hard shaft leaking against Fin's thigh, and his sweaty, musky scent that was so clearly masculine. Fin hadn't anticipated how much he'd love the obvious differences between Vaughn and his former female lovers. He gave Vaughn's shoulder a sharp nip. "Come on. Don't be a tease."

"Am not." Vaughn sat up and leaned toward the nightstand. "Seems you're impatient while I'm trying to be romantic."

"Romantic?" Fin watched Vaughn retrieve the lube and open it with his thumb. "And that from the man who wants me to tongue his balls. Although I have to admit I have a lot to learn when it comes to blow jobs and stuff."

Vaughn coated his fingers with lube. "I'm always available for training purposes. You can lick and suck every inch of me, kitten. Now . . . about your legs."

Fin threw his legs over Vaughn's shoulders and wriggled around. "Do I need a pillow for under my butt?"

"Have you found more interesting details during your online research?" He leaned back down and licked through the valley between Fin's pecs. "Curious minds want to know. We can try everything you're interested in." When Vaughn trailed his lubed fingers over Fin's balls and the soft skin behind them, Fin shuddered. He closed his lips over Finley's nipple and sucked hard.

Fin arched his back. "Fuck, V!" The warm suction, along with the roughness of Vaughn's tongue as he flicked it over the hardened nub, drove him crazy. "I'm . . . obviously a nipple guy."

"And I'll take full advantage of that fact." Vaughn rubbed a slippery finger across Fin's hole and switched to the other nipple, giving it the same attention.

Fin was so overwhelmed by the feelings Vaughn elicited that he didn't notice Vaughn increasing the pressure until a finger slipped inside him. Growling quietly, he clutched

Vaughn's biceps. "Damn. This will sting, huh?" Not that he'd back out of the claiming. As far as Fin was concerned, they were equal partners. He wouldn't think of suggesting Vaughn bottom all the time, either — he could take it. "Always wondered . . ."

Vaughn gave a short laugh. "You wondered about gay sex? I'll make sure you're ready to take me, but I won't lie. The first time is always a little —"

Fin kissed the rest of the sentence away. "Of course I was curious. Many of my friends are gay or bi. Add another finger." While he tried to relax into Vaughn's naughty caresses, he tousled Vaughn's beautiful hair. When Vaughn touched something inside him, Fin thought the top of his head would blow off. He fisted the red strands and rolled his hips. "Damn!"

"Hmm. *That's* the spot." A devilish grin curled Vaughn's lip. "Could probably make you come by rubbing your prostate and sucking you."

Fin shuddered. "Maybe for the second round." The heat between them was so intense their skin was slick and slippery. His legs kept sliding from Vaughn's shoulders until Vaughn grabbed them and looped them around his hips. Gradually, he felt himself relax around Vaughn's thrusting fingers.

Vaughn licked the sweat off Fin's chest where it was still bruised from the assassin's bullet. Fin's dog tags dangled from Vaughn's neck and dragged across Fin's skin. "You feel so hot, so tight." He added a third finger. "Enjoy the stretch?"

Why did Vaughn insist on holding a conversation while they were in the throes of passion? He pushed down on Vaughn's digits, trying to get more friction, more pressure on his prostate. "*Please. Fuck* me already!" Fin grunted when Vaughn slid his fingers from his ass. He watched Vaughn reach down and rub his slick hand over his impressive length.

"Tell me if you need a break." Vaughn brushed his lips over Finley's and moved his body sensually against Fin's.

Fin never broke his mate's gaze while Vaughn pressed the smooth, slick head of his cock against his entrance. The pressure increased and became uncomfortable, until the tip finally popped inside and forced a grunt from Fin's throat.

Above him, Vaughn started to tremble. The muscles in his arms and chest tensed and released repeatedly. His breathing sped up while he held his hips absolutely still. Vaughn closed his eyes, letting out a moan that was both pain and pleasure.

Fin pulled him into a kiss, nipped and licked Vaughn's lips until the man opened up and met his tongue. He slid his hands over Vaughn's hard shoulders in a soothing caress.

"*I* should be the one comforting *you*." Vaughn let out a panted laugh. He hissed and cursed when Finley laughed. "Shit. Don't do that."

Fin tipped his head back and urged Vaughn to rest his forehead against his. "You can go on. Give me more." Feeling Vaughn enter his body was, hands down, the oddest thing he'd ever felt. Yes, it hurt a little, but it also stimulated nerves he'd never known he had. Fin panted through the strain and breathed a sigh of relief when he felt Vaughn's balls against his ass. "Thought for a second your dick was endless," he teased.

Vaughn snorted. "So many naughty replies in my head. Are you okay?"

Fin tightened his legs around Vaughn's waist. "Hmhm. Move. Show me why so many men and women do this."

"With pleasure." Vaughn undulated his hips, pushing into Fin, although Fin was sure he couldn't get any deeper, before he slowly pulled back.

Fin gasped as fireworks went off inside him. Out was good. Fuck, out was *very* good. And Vaughn moved so cruelly slowly, so carefully, that Fin wanted to slap him upside the head. Instead he tugged at Vaughn's locks and cried out. "*Yesssss*. Right there."

Vaughn chuckled, his next thrust more forceful. "You'll feel it when I'm *right there*." He placed his hands on the back of Finley's thighs, pushing them closer to his chest. Then he picked up the pace.

Pinned in place, Fin was reduced to feeling. Vaughn's harsh thrust caused a delicious burn. The scent of sex hung heavy in the air. Combined with their grunts and the wet slap of skin against skin, Fin's balls tightened painfully.

"Close! V, *please*. Bite me." He slung his fingers around Vaughn's ball chain necklace and tugged sharply.

Vaughn growled, the sound pure animal. "Come for me. I want to feel your ass squeeze my cock. I want you to lose it without the bite." He canted his hips, and suddenly Fin knew what Vaughn had meant saying he'd know when Vaughn was *right there*.

His mate was out to kill him. Helpless against Vaughn pummeling his prostate, he tried to tighten the muscles in his channel and was rewarded by a low, drawn-out moan. But then Vaughn reached between them and curled his hand around Fin's shaft and it was over. His orgasm slammed into him and made him see stars. Spunk splattered his chest and caught in the red pelt on Vaughn's belly. It went on and on until his balls hurt and he needed Vaughn to stop nudging his gland.

Vaughn shoved deep and froze over him. His muscles twitched, and a ragged sob escaped his lips while he filled Fin's channel with heat.

Fuck, that feels good.

"*Claim me!*" Fin didn't care if he sounded desperate. He yanked and pulled at his mate until Vaughn fell on top of him and bit the soft flesh over his shoulder. Another mini-orgasm rocked through him. Fin felt wrung out, a hypersensitive bundle of raw nerves. Although Vaughn was heavy, Fin cherished his mate's comforting weight. Nobody could touch him while the big lug covered him. He lifted his hand and stroked the back of Vaughn's head, purring quietly.

Vaughn didn't move, save for pulling his teeth from Fin's flesh and licking over the oozing wound. He nuzzled the side of Fin's neck and sniffed him. "Love you."

"I love you, too. That. Was. Spectacular."

"I didn't hurt you?" Vaughn asked quietly. "I was scared shitless I'd fuck up your first time."

Fin shook his head. "Nah. Why so self-conscious?"

"Because, for all my haughty talk, I've never topped before."

Fin gasped. "You . . . but . . . what?"

Vaughn kissed his cheek and snuggled in. "Walter was much older than me and he didn't like bottoming. After his death, I couldn't bring myself to hook up with anyone. I didn't say anything because I was . . . embarrassed."

"You were embarrassed to tell me, an anal-virgin, that you've never pitched?" Fin laughed.

"Sounds dumb when you say it like that." Vaughn hummed. "I can feel you and your cougar. Your happiness. Your love." He carefully slid from Fin's body and rolled to the side.

Fin winced at the separation. He turned on his side, curling against Vaughn's solid body. "Want to know what I feel? Seed leaking out of my ass. Kinda weird." He reached behind himself and slid his fingers through his crack, moaning when they brushed over his tender hole. "Okay, it's also hot." He met Vaughn's amused gaze and winked.

"Give me a second and I'll fetch us a washcloth. My legs are cooked noodles." He pecked Fin's lips, but soon the peck turned into a slow, thorough, and downright dirty duel of tongues.

Fin forgot all about washcloths as he clutched Vaughn's

shoulders and rolled on top of him. Cleaning up had to wait. He had a feeling they'd get dirty again soon anyway.

CHAPTER THIRTEEN

Vaughn felt a sense of déjà vu as he sat beside Finley at Xander's conference table. Bailey and Romeo were talking quietly at the other end of the table, bent over Romeo's laptop.

Malcolm sat on Vaughn's other side and chatted with Jaxon. "Come on. It's a couple of beers," Malcolm cajoled. He raked his fingers through hair more orange than red, resembling the fur of his rare golden tiger.

Jaxon crossed his leanly muscled arms over his chest. He looked torn. "I don't know, Mal. Viggo was secretive earlier. I think he might have something planned for us. I don't want to ruin one of his rare attempts at romance."

Mal playfully tugged at the end of Jaxon's long black braid. "Aww. Don't leave me hanging. Djimon is with Kei and his kids all the time. Fin fell into Vaughn's clutches, and Alan . . ." He grabbed a chocolate from the plate in the middle of the table and threw it at Alan. The beta reached up and caught the sweet ammunition without looking up and stuffed his mouth. "Alan's an old bore."

Vaughn's research had proved Alan David Abramowitz was a righteous, highly ethical man who always had his alpha's back. And although he was strong and able to hold his own in a battle, his job was slightly different than that of the betas in Vaughn's home pack. Alan filled in for Xander whenever the alpha was away. He handled the pride's finances and was the person pride members turned to with their problems. As Vaughn understood it, Alan was a buffer between Xander and the pride.

The system seemed to work. From what Vaughn had observed, the pride loved Alan for his fairness and his funny, teasing disposition.

Alan flipped Malcolm the bird. He threw his tablet on the table and stretched. "Ask Bailey." Mischief twinkled in Alan's eyes. "Doc might be in the mood for a sip after work." He made slurping sounds.

While Malcolm squinted at Alan, Bailey snorted. "The nineties called, Alan. They want their jokes back."

Finley leaned around Vaughn. "Hey, Alan. Any news from your sister yet?"

Alan sighed. "Nope. I've been a freaking mess ever since Thony donated. My man has his cell with him constantly in case Janie calls us with news. Yesterday he nearly showered with the thing."

Vaughn had no idea what he was talking about. "Donated what?"

Djimon flopped into the chair beside Alan, the biggest damn coffee mug Vaughn had ever seen clutched in his hand. "His swimmers. Thony convinced Alan to start a family. He has no idea what he's getting himself into." He took a long, slurping sip of coffee and groaned. "Today I woke up with a toy elephant tangled in my hair. Took Kei thirty minutes to free it. He found a couple more gray hairs as well."

Vaughn winced in sympathy. The tall African American man had black corkscrew locks down to his waist. That had to hurt.

Alan scoffed. "Well, you had to overdo it and have triplets. And Thony didn't talk me into anything. It was *our* decision."

Jaxon snickered. "Of course it was."

Djimon gave Alan a tired look. "Aren't cats known for multiples?"

Alan blanched and sputtered. "Only in the animal

kingdom." He shuddered. "Well, at least I won't be the one giving birth to them."

"Nope. You let your poor sister do the hard work." Djimon smirked. "Baby beta."

Before Alan could reply, Xander rapped his knuckles on the table. "All right. Bailey and Romeo prepared a presentation. Romeo successfully decoded whatever Finley and Vaughn stole from the lab. Show's yours." He sat down and swiveled his chair toward the men.

Romeo pushed his glasses up his nose and clicked away on his laptop. Bailey stood beside him, clearing his throat. "First, we'll show you some pictures. During the last meeting I mentioned two other assassin teams. Romeo and I collected the basic info along with their photos so you'll recognize them right away." He nodded at Romeo, who clicked and activated the large screen.

The pictures of five men popped up instantly. Beside the photos Vaughn saw their birth dates, their profession before they entered the program, as well as the field they specialized in with the assassin squad. These were the five guys Bailey had mentioned during the last meeting. Thorne Wilder was one of them. Vaughn hadn't seen him yet because he refused to return to Pumpkin Creek Pack.

Bailey pointed at the grim-looking black man. "This is Wilder, who currently resides with Donavan's coyotes." While Bailey explained the men's training, Vaughn concentrated on the other four guys. Aside from Thorne, there was one other African American—Priest Cavendish, the paramedic. Cross Shepherd and Kee Bishop were Caucasians, Cross a blond like Aaron, and Bishop with short brown hair. Lance Darwin appeared to be of Middle Eastern heritage, with a Roman nose, swarthy skin, and black hair.

Vaughn snapped back to the presentation when Romeo cleared his throat. "The stolen files were enlightening.

Although we don't know the chemical process of turning a shifter's blood into the potion that changed Bailey and his comrades, we now have detailed information about the human guinea pigs, including those who died during the process. Means we know how many assassins we're dealing with and their specific abilities and training. Although the whole operation is hush-hush, Taylor is a stickler for order and a thorough professional when it comes to his test subjects. Everything was neatly catalogued."

Bailey nodded. "My team was Team One. That no longer exists. Thorne leads Team Two. This is Team Three." He clicked a button on Romeo's laptop. Five other pictures popped up. The men looked military through and through, with their buzz cuts and stern expressions. Vaughn memorized their names and faces. Their abilities matched those of Team Two, which didn't surprise Vaughn.

"How many teams are we talking about?" Xander asked.

"Two more, according to Taylor's files." Bailey sighed. "These are newer, the assassins turned not more than two years ago. And they're mixed groups, both males and females. One team's assigned to the facility Vaughn and Fin visited." He looked at Vaughn. "You killed one of them. Do you recognize her?" Bailey clicked again and more pictures appeared.

Beside him, Fin gasped and touched his arm. "Olivia Storey. That's her."

Bailey sighed again. "I have more bad news. Aside from the teams, we're dealing with ten other individuals who work solo. God knows where they are right now."

Vaughn nodded, closing his hand over Finley's trembling fingers on his arm. "Romeo, anything from her phone?"

"Nope. It was a burner phone. She received a single call, but I can't track it. She was from Oregon. Twenty-six years old. Suffering from terminal cancer when Taylor found her."

Romeo rubbed his temples. "This is rubbish. If we were in the city, I'd hack the CCTV and write a neat face-recognition program to alert us if any of those yahoos were around. But we're in the middle of nowhere. Whoever wants to reach us through the official roads has to go through Green Valley. But the town doesn't have traffic lights, much less CCTV. Fuck. It's hacker hell."

Bailey sat down and leaned over the table, grabbing an orange from the fruit basket sitting in the middle. "The town's small." He sat down as he started peeling the fruit. "But you're right. We need a warning system."

Malcolm's eyes were wide. "You mean you can do all that shit? I thought you . . . fix laptops and stuff."

Romeo shot the man a peeved look. "Just because I removed the viruses from your laptop that you caught from watching too much porn doesn't mean—"

"All right." Xander raised his hand. "Enough. Romeo, you can wire the surrounding woods. Give Alan a cost estimate, but please don't go overboard. And maybe I can help with something else. Sterling won the election for police chief over in Green Valley." He grinned when loud clapping ensued. "Yeah, he's ecstatic. He promised he'd bring up the lack of surveillance to Mayor Willis. If she agrees, Sterling said he'd ask you to head the project. As always, it's a money issue."

Romeo clapped his hands like a giddy child on Christmas. He turned to Jules and started murmuring rapidly.

Vaughn leaned against his mate and lowered his voice. "Sterling?"

"He's a caracal shifter who's been part of the police department in Green Valley since he moved to Wildcat Hills seven years ago." Finley smiled. "I'm happy he won the election. Hunter Sterling is an upright guy. Opened the police department for two other pride members who work as officers."

Vaughn made a mental note to grill Romeo for intel on the

new chief and start his own investigation about the Green Valley Police Department. Wildcat Hills Pride was his new home, and he'd leave nothing to chance. Especially not the safety of his mate. "I'll help Ro. I'm good with surveillance." He winked at his friend.

"Cool. On another note," Romeo piped up. "I contacted a hacker buddy who also works for the government on occasion." He swiveled to look at Xander. "We'll have air monitoring for Taylor's lab in a couple of days."

Vaughn's eyes widened. "How?"

"If I tell you, I'll have to kill you." Romeo grinned. "My friend has access to satellites. He agreed to help us."

Xander frowned. "Illegal access? Tell him to be careful, okay? We don't want him to risk his life."

Bailey nodded. "Xander's right, Romeo. Angering the government is fucking dangerous." He slid a slice of orange into his mouth and offered another to Jules, who stared at the fruit hungrily.

"Is your friend aware of shifters?" Xander asked.

"Yes. He's human, but his mom mated with a wolf shifter. Our secret is safe. And he's exceptionally good at what he does."

Malcolm wrinkled his nose. "Wolves . . ."

Finley let out a warning growl. "My mate is a coyote shifter, so bite your tongue if you planned to make a *cats versus dogs* joke."

Malcolm raised his hands with a grin on his face. "Hey, I have nothing against coyotes. They're kinda the cute, cuddly version of wolves."

"I'll give you cuddly." Vaughn growled.

Alan snorted. "Mal, you better find someone to suck your cock later at the bar. You've been even more of a prick than usual lately."

"And you think my mood is related to not getting laid? My

cock and I are well taken care of, thank you very much." Malcolm turned up his nose in what Vaughn had always thought of as a pissed-off-cat gesture.

Snickering, Finley snatched a banana from the basket and waved it around. "Are you kidding? Tense and growly has been your default setting lately. How Bailey managed not to kill you while living with you is a mystery."

Vaughn watched his mate peel the banana and lift it to his mouth. A deep growl escaped his lips when Fin closed his lips around the tip. Malcolm's snort drew his attention off the cock-hardening sight. "What?"

"Look who needs to have his dick sucked." The tiger shifter licked his teeth. "It's not me drooling over a man eating a banana."

"Not this time," Romeo muttered.

Malcolm shot his ex a sharp look, his face blushing a dark pink. Finley's cheeks were flushed as well, but he didn't look embarrassed. Instead, Fin licked up his snack before he took another slow bite, winking at Vaughn.

Xander pinched the bridge of his nose. "Romeo, anything else I need to know about the files?"

"Oh . . ." Romeo scratched his head. "I found messages between Thoreau and Taylor. I'll forward them to you. It's mostly private stuff, but they might come in handy at a later date."

"Fine. Meeting dismissed. I need sleep and a dose of my mate. And maybe three years of vacation on a remote beach." Xander groaned as he pushed from his chair. "Raine and Armand are expected back from Pumpkin Creek tomorrow or the day after. Let's wait and see what they find out."

Everyone at the table jumped when the door flew open and Asa hurried into the room, one of Kei's adorable kids perched on his hip. He held a cell with a neon yellow rubber sleeve in his hand that he thrust at Xander. The poor guy was deadly pale. "It's Don. There's been an incident."

Xander grabbed the phone and stood quickly. "Don?"

Asa turned toward the table as he clutched the baby tighter against his chest. "Thorne Wilder escaped from his cell approximately ten minutes ago."

Bailey cursed and brought his fist so hard on the table Vaughn feared the wood might crack. "How the hell did that happen?"

Vaughn wrapped his arm around Fin's shoulders and pulled him into the curve of his body. This was bad news. Vaughn had no doubt Wilder would return with his teammates and take revenge on the Pumpkin Creek Pack for his imprisonment.

"That's not the worst." Asa swallowed, his Adam's apple bobbing. "The guards who found his cell empty said there was a puddle of blood on the floor. It's from Raine Cosworth. He's missing."

YOU MAY ALSO ENJOY THE FOLLOWING FROM EXTASY BOOKS INC:

Anthony's Tailor
Liza Kay

Excerpt

Oh my God, Trisha! What have you done? Aiden Fox stood, a tad dumbfounded, in the only five-star hotel in town, feeling as though he'd wandered right into the middle of one of those fancy Russian Fabergé eggs. Thank God he'd parked the beat-up piece of crap he called his car at the back of the hotel. The body was more than a little rusty. No need to scare the nobles with his deathtrap of a car.

For a tailor such as Aiden, the hotel represented heaven. Shades of gold, bronze, and pearl surrounded him. He walked beneath glittering crystal chandeliers over a thick, golden-yellow carpet. Heavy brocade drapes in slightly paler shades covered the windows. Unfortunately, he didn't have time to admire the interior design.

Aiden winced when he rounded a corner and fifty shades of pink assaulted his retinas. A sure sign Patricia "Trisha" Wintash, his client, had caused havoc among those posh halls. Or, more likely, her decoration crew was to blame. Even out-and-proud Aiden thought the décor too flamboyant and excessive.

He shuddered and walked farther down the hallway. His mission was to find a surely hysterical Trisha and rescue her perfect wedding dress. Brides were unpredictable by definition. God knew he'd be a nervous wreck, too, if he ever managed to catch a man willing to marry him.

Aiden loved to care for his clients, but Trisha's teary emergency call that afternoon had thrown his plans for a lazy day on his sofa into disarray. For months, Aiden had sat at the sewing machine with the damn dress, working overtime in his little tailor shop to finish it right in time for the wedding. Now she had an imaginary problem—just what it was Aiden hadn't been able to filter from her rambling—with the wickedly expensive creation of silk and lace.

Convincing her that she looked perfect, adorable, and like the most beautiful bride ever was on the top of Aiden's priority list. Trisha would love him, her daddy would love that his little girl was happy and smiling again, and Aiden would receive a splendid recommendation which would help his business. Win-win situation.

A wedding like Trisha's, with both bride and groom belonging to the upper crust of Maryland, was the opportunity to gain new and well-off clients. Aiden desperately needed some good news right now. He'd opened his shop a year ago, and each day was a small struggle for success and independence.

Money was tight. Although he always managed to feed himself and his fat cat, Button, some months he barely scraped by. His private life? Oh, boy. Despair, thy name is Aiden.

A few steps ahead of him, a door opened, and he could hear Trisha's nasal voice. Please let me solve her problem quickly. The noise level coming from the room increased as a man stepped out into the hallway, and suddenly Aiden was eye to eye with . . ."Anthony?"

Aiden came to an immediate halt, his feet glued to the

thousand-dollar carpet. He stared openmouthed at the man he thought he'd never see again. Dressed in a stunning tuxedo that was maybe a tad stuffy, but which suited his tall frame, he looked the same as the night of their disastrous dinner but . . . totally different.

The hot guy had sauntered into his shop a month ago. Aiden had always had a soft spot for tall, dark, and handsome. Add a pair of light brown eyes and Aiden had been swooning. However, Anthony had turned out to be a real prick. Aiden had severed all contact with Anthony after their last date. Why were handsome guys always straight or assholes?

Aiden's face flushed hot. "Anthony?" he asked again. Inwardly, he cursed the fact his voice wasn't as steady as he'd have liked it to be.

Anthony faced him, his expression changing from clearly exhausted to questioning. "Yes? May I help you?" He added a raised eyebrow to his puzzled question. His voice sounded different. It held a soft timbre Aiden had never heard from him before. Smooth, like honey.

Aiden felt his knees turn to jelly. Stupid. He was stupid, no other explanation needed. Anthony was a douche, a bastard who'd played with him just to find a way into his pants. Aiden shouldn't be drooling over Mr. Dark and Sexy. He was a bit taken aback by his strong reaction.

It wasn't much, but Aiden scraped up the last morsels of his battered dignity and pulled back his shoulders. "What are you doing here? Are you a friend of the Wintash family?"

Anthony now turned his whole body to face him and took two steps forward. "I'm sorry? Do we know each other?"

The bastard had the guts to act as though they'd never met before? Aiden scoffed. "You think you're one hell of an actor, huh?" Aiden fisted his hands on his hips. "Look, it's no big deal. We dated, it didn't work out. No hard feelings. But there's no reason for you to act as though we don't know each other. You're not a celebrity who needs to be afraid of his reputation." Okay, maybe he'd snapped the last word. Maybe he'd even glowered at the sexy guy.

Instead of snapping back, Anthony remained polite. "This is a misunderstanding. I apologize, but now isn't the best moment for a conversation. My brother will be getting married in two hours, I hope, and the bride is . . ." He trailed off and waved his hand dismissively.

Aiden hated it when people avoided arguments by staying cool and collected. Faced with so much bullshit, Aiden was at the end of his tether. "Are you fucking kidding me?" Oops. These halls had one hell of an echo. Aiden quickly clapped his hand over his mouth, knowing he was getting redder with every moment that passed. Not a good color for his fair complexion. Aiden rarely lost control. At least, not in public places. "Sorry—"

The next shock jolted Aiden to the core when another man joined him and Anthony in the corridor. The second man made him wonder whether his grandmother had spiked her cookies again. He'd told her to stop adding the damn weed when she hosted her women's nights.

There, right next to Anthony, stood a second Anthony. In a perfectly tailored, fucking wedding suit.

"Anthony?" Aiden whispered and tried not to freak out. Although nobody could blame him under the circumstances. Seriously, two Anthonies stood right in front of him! The first one with a puzzled, but friendly twinkle in his sherry-colored eyes. Anthony the second's face wore a hard, angry expression. Both men looked almost the same, but the particular hardness on Anthony the second's face Aiden knew all too well. He'd seen it on occasion during their dates.

With an uneasy feeling coiling in the pit of his stomach, Aiden tried to put the unknown pieces together and turned to the first Anthony. Obviously, the guy was the twin he hadn't known about. Aiden hoped for an easy explanation. However, when he looked into those friendly, caring, and concerned eyes, he knew easy explanations weren't on the menu today. It hit him like a truck crashing into his crappy old car.

The first man's name might be Anthony, but the guy he'd dated was, without a doubt, the one wearing the wedding suit.

Aiden had, unknowingly, dated Trisha's fiancé.

ABOUT THE AUTHOR

Liza grew up in a tiny village in Germany, the kind where you know everybody and everybody knows you. She migrated to a bigger town to attend college, although her parents often wonder if she really moved out. Now, with a degree in her pocket, she's perfectly capable of working as a librarian. Never one to do what's expected of her, Liza currently browses different branches of employment.

She started writing in college when she found herself unable to ignore the guys living in her head any longer, and to distract herself from the stifling, non-fiction stuff taught in class. Liza is really fond of the dudes whispering in her mind—no matter if handsome or flawed, big or small, sulky or easy-going. They all deserve love and their HEAs.

When she's not writing, you can find her curled up with a good book and a cup of tea, a cat in her lap, or a camera at the ready.

You can contact her at onelizakay@gmail.com
Or visit her blog at https://onelizakay.wordpress.com/

www.ingramcontent.com/pod-product-compliance
Lightning Source LLC
Chambersburg PA
CBHW060827120626
46557CB00001B/401